I0717676

To Hell
and Back

DEMELZA CARLTON

DEDICATION

One

"You're coming with me, Luce. We'll return to HELL together."

Luce watched the chainmail-clad girl clink off. Armour on a guy just looks old-fashioned, but on a woman…it made him feel a bit nostalgic. If Mel had fought in the Heavenly Battle all those centuries ago dressed in mail like that one…Hell, he'd have fallen to his knees and begged to surrender to her. Maybe if he hinted to Mel, she'd consider…

"Just think – you'll get to wear pants again."

Pants. Damn. That meant no fooling

around. At least, not yet.

"Any chance you'll let me lose the pants later?" he asked eagerly.

"Luce."

Two

"It looks just like we left it," Luce said, looking around as he headed for the bedroom. He stumbled over a shoe and kicked it away, swearing. "Who left all these here, where I could trip over them?"

"They're yours, Luce. You were wearing them when you kicked the juvenile swan and earned yourself a nasty nip, back at the office Christmas party," Mel replied, stepping daintily over the obstacles as she made her way to the kitchen. "Would you like some tea? I find it always helps ground me when I've been without a body for a while."

"Sure," Luce said, grinning. "Boil the kettle. I've been thinking about your body all week and I have some ideas I'd like to try out." He pulled out a dining chair and sat down, patting his lap. "We could get started while the water heats up. Maybe heat things up a little more."

Mel laughed, crossing the kitchen to fill the kettle. She clicked it on, returned to Luce, and lowered herself onto his lap, crossing her wrists behind his neck. "I have some ideas, too," she murmured, drawing him in closer for a kiss.

His hands caressed her back through the silk of her dress and his arms tightened around her as she slipped her tongue between his lips. Mel could feel the love spilling out of his soul and hoped he could feel the same from hers. So many centuries of soul-reading without revealing her presence…but she was learning to let Luce sense her.

Her body betrayed her thoughts, making Luce break the kiss to whisper, "You're too tense, Mel. Don't think about it. Only share what you want to. Your body is expressive enough for me to read plenty from you, without you needing to share your whole soul. Humans manage love like this just fine." He chuckled. "Focus on my body for once and not my soul. I made sure it was perfect for you, Mel. I promise you'll enjoy it." He pressed his lips to the side of her neck, trailing kisses down to the neckline of her dress.

Mel tipped her head back, closing her eyes as he kissed her breasts – or what little he could reach without her taking her clothes off. "Luce, I'd like to…"

"So would I," he said, returning to her lips. He deepened the kiss, tightening his hold on her as if he'd never, ever let her go.

A new and distinctly annoyed voice rang out, killing the moment. "Kissing demons is disgusting, Mel. I didn't believe you'd ever…"

"If the lady will let me, I'll show you just how wrong you are," Luce offered instantly.

"No, Luce, that's not…" Mel pulled away from him. "Raphael, you should really knock first. You could have saved yourself from seeing things you don't like. You'd best remember to be polite to my guest, too – Luce is an angel, the same as you. Definitely not a demon any more."

"Fine. Former demon, then. You look like you're about to…sleep with him! Ex-demon or not, I wouldn't have thought you'd stoop so low as to…"

"Low is condemning an innocent man to Hell, Raphael," Mel said coldly. "What Luce and I do is really none of your business, nor your concern. Why are you here? If you've only come to lecture me on going to Hell and bringing Luce home with me, you may leave." Gracefully, she rose from Luce's lap and headed for the kitchen, smoothing her dress down along the way.

"I came here to tell you about Persi and the mess she's left us in. It has nothing to do with him." Raphael glared at Luce. "He's the one you should ask to leave."

Mel spooned tea into her teapot. "Luce is my guest and he's free to leave whenever he wishes, but he's here at my invitation now. My love, I think you should stay to hear what Raphael has to say."

"Why?" Raphael spat.

Mel poured a steady stream of hot water over the mixture of leaves and flowers. "Because I need Luce to help me clean up Persi's mess. He's going to return to his old job as CEO of the HELL Corporation."

"WHAT?" the two men shouted together.

Luce recovered first from his shock. "Only if you're working there, too. I'm not going back to HELL without a small slice of Heaven. You can have the office across from mine and I'll make you coffee every morning."

Mel's smile lit up her whole face. "That sounds lovely. Of course I will, Luce."

Three

Mel carried her cup of tea to the armchair by the window and settled into the well-padded cushions. Luce clunked his cup on the coffee table and sprawled across the sofa, leaving Raphael the other armchair. He watched in fascination as the archangel dragged one of the dining chairs over and parked his backside on that instead. He sat stiff and silent, making Luce wonder if he was going to say anything at all or if he was just wasting their time.

"Raphael, didn't you come here to tell me

about Persi?" Mel asked. "I mean, do you know who the last person was to see her before she disappeared?"

"Me," he said hoarsely, then cleared his throat. "Me. I was the last one to see her. We were discussing the dismantling of the demon corporation and their banishment back to Hell. Persephone worried about sending anyone back, because that would only strengthen this guy's army." He shot Luce a cold glare. "He was pining for you, she said, but he'd soon realise you wouldn't have feelings for the likes of him and take up arms against Heaven again. I told Persephone that she'd have some time, as the devil had managed to lure you into Hell and under some sort of spell that made you forget who and what he is." Raphael's eyes glittered. "She said –"

"Hang on," Luce interrupted. "You fed her a line of bullshit about how I've worked some sort of hocus pocus on Mel? I thought angels couldn't lie."

Raphael glared at him again. "I don't know how you did it, but there's no way Mel would give you the time of day without some sort of magic. Persephone said she'd find you and make it right. But instead, she disappeared." He dropped his gaze to the floor. "She was supposed to visit her mother in Heaven after our meeting, but she never arrived. Demeter said Persephone would never have forgotten – she's very close to her mother."

The same mother who'd tried to take a sword to me, Luce fumed.

"If he wasn't with you at the time, Mel, I'd have suspected him," Raphael continued. "After what he did to Persi last time –"

Luce jumped to his feet. "I didn't touch the little bitch! She's feeding lies to the lot of you. Say it to my face, angel. If you want to accuse me of crimes I didn't commit, we can take this all the way to Heaven's gates. Go on!" He advanced on the wide-eyed angel – or at least he tried to, but he couldn't seem to move.

Raphael rose. "Not so tough now, are you?" he taunted, yet when he tried to step forward, it looked like he'd run into an invisible wall.

"Enough," Mel said softly, her eyes darting from Raphael to Luce and back again. The edge of steel in her tone made it an order neither of them could disobey. And neither of them could move…

She was doing it. Luce realised a split second before Raphael did.

"Whatever you believe about Luce, you're mistaken," she said to Raphael. "Do you know anything else about Persi?"

"No," he said sullenly. "So I should go." He attempted to, but Mel's invisible grip still held him fast.

Luce grinned. "Now who's tough?"

Mel placed her hand on his chest. "Luce, please. The more polite you both are, the more smoothly this will go and the sooner it'll be over. Now, I want both of you to sit down, please."

Luce finally capitulated and, a moment later, Raphael followed.

"Better," Mel said. "So, I gather that the problem is that Persi's missing and no one's in charge of Hell. Yes?"

"No," Luce replied. "I think Lili and the other senior demons are in charge. The HELL Corporation could be run by a concussed monkey right now, for all I know. I only signed over the company to the nephilim girl."

Mel inclined her head. "Okay. So no one's in charge of the HELL Corporation and the best qualified person to replace her is the retired CEO – you, Luce. As we've already agreed, I'll assist. Raphael, if you find Persi, or if someone else does, you already said she's looking for me, so I want to know if you hear anything about her."

Raphael nodded, but the calculating look in his eyes showed that his mind was working overtime. "I'll give you regular updates about anything we hear to do with Persi."

"I also want a team of angels to assist me in the office, with some Exousiai, if George can spare any."

"Oh no, not bloody Powers!" Luce groaned. "Last time I ran into one of them, he pulled out a damn sword and tried to butcher me in the middle of the street. The last thing I need in HELL is a bunch of archaic warrior angels who think I have a target painted on my arse."

"Wearing pants might help fix that problem, Luce." Mel's eyes danced with laughter before she resumed in a more serious tone, "Exousiai are experts at dealing with demons, so I need some. I'm sorry. But Raphael can explain the terms – no drawing without provocation and they must stay away from you. I'll give you a list of who I want, Raphael."

Raphael nodded again. "Is that all?"

"No," Mel said slowly. "There's also the matter of the underwear you owe me. And a new shirt."

Luce smirked at Raphael, only to find the angel wore a similar expression. So who owed her underwear, then?

"Raphael, I was helping out the Agency when my clothing was damaged. I require replacements," Mel explained.

Luce sniggered.

"I'm not…not shopping for women's clothes!" Raphael spluttered, flushing.

Mel shrugged. "Fine." She held out her hand. "Then give me your Agency credit card, please."

Raphael pulled out his wallet and handed over the card, glowering. "He better not be helping you."

A wicked smile spread across her face.

"That's none of your business, Raphael. Now, if there's nothing else…keep me updated. I'll see you out."

When the door closed behind Raphael, Luce said, "I can help you. I know this shop that sells the sexiest —"

"Luce. Though I don't do it often, I'm familiar with clothes shopping. I'm sure I'll be fine. Besides, I have to do something on my lunch break and there are plenty of suitable stores in the city near the office." Mel's eyes met his. "Now, what were we planning on doing before we were interrupted?"

Luce grinned. "Let me refresh your memory."

Four

Luce's heart sank as each step dragged him deeper inside the HELL Corporation building. Was it dread, sadness or something else that made him want to be anywhere but here? He couldn't decide. All he knew for sure was that there was no place for him in Hell or HELL any more. He was a changed man…demon…no, angel; happy to follow wherever his sweet angel led.

Mel stepped into the darkened CEO's office first. "She's not here and she hasn't been for a while."

Luce edged in behind her and flicked the lights on. She was right, of course – there was no sign of the half-angel here. Just thinking about her made him shiver, though he couldn't be sure if there was some sign of her presence or whether he was just imagining things.

"Oh, she left the paintings!" Mel cried, crossing the room to stand before the framed Pro Hart landscapes. "I've wanted to take a closer look at these since the first time I visited your office."

Luce racked his memory, trying to recall when she'd expressed her interest in his taste for Australian art. His heart sank when he realised that on that long-ago day, he'd completely ignored her wish to know more about him as he'd let his own carnal desire to possess her consume him. Oh Hell, he'd been so cocksure she'd obey him, he'd unzipped his pants the moment he heard her voice.

He'd never be able to make amends for that, but he'd go a long way to try.

"They're yours if you want them. I picked them not just for the colours, but for the life they represent. The friendly games of cricket on the beach, the rugby matches, the country towns with people and red dirt and gum trees…it's the idealised life Australians want to live, even when they can't. I wish I could show you the Rembrandts I used to have in my house in Amsterdam – full of angelic merchants, when the reality was that they were waging war on the native inhabitants of the countries they'd invaded and killing their own employees with disease and malnutrition to feed their own greed. So much easier to get them to sign their souls away when they believed they were behaving more like angels than demons…" He became conscious of her concerned eyes on him. "You should have them. Every time I look at them now, I'll remember how I corrupted this or that politician, company director or angel in this office."

Mel kissed his cheek. "No, we'll leave temptation here, so I can see them every time I come visit you in your office. We can admire them together."

His heart ached to do something else for

her, something that would wipe away the painful memories of his first misguided advances. When she'd politely declined and walked out on him, leaving behind the intoxicating scent that drove him mad. A crazy, half-formed idea came to him and he opened the cupboard before he could talk himself out of it. Everything was just as he'd left it – Persephone hadn't touched anything on this shelf.

Luce grabbed the spray bottle and roll of paper towels, bumping the door shut with his elbow as he turned back to the desk. The bottle squeaked as he squirted cleaning fluid all over the desk surface, but he continued until he'd covered it completely. He set the bottle down and ripped off a length of towelling, swiping at the desk until it shone.

Doubt seized him. She'd refuse him again, he was certain of it. Plus, Persephone had used this desk in his absence – one wipe wasn't enough. He spritzed the surface again and repeated his furious circles with the paper towels. A second time – did it need a third? It had to be perfect for Mel – she deserved no less. Luce lifted the bottle again and pulled back the trigger.

"What are you doing?"

Luce wasn't sure how long Mel's eyes had been on him, but they held sadness. She was going to refuse. She was going to remember how horrible he'd been when she'd first started working here, change her mind and never come back. She'd…

Mel gently pulled the ammonia-drenched paper towels from his hand and dropped them in the wastepaper basket under the desk. "It's clean. You were very thorough. I'm sure you don't need to worry about working on a dirty desk ever again. You can ask Mephi to send a reminder to the office cleaners first thing –"

"No," Luce blurted out. "I cleaned it for you. I want…I NEED you to lie down on the desk."

She stepped back, out of his reach. Luce's heart died a little. "Luce, for your own good, you know I have to say no to that. I know this office reminds you of what you were in the past, but you're a different man now, and you can't just give in to your desires and passions the way you used to. If you really feel you need me that badly, you can stay at my place tonight and perhaps we can –"

"Melody, please. I've changed, but I'm still the same man. One who regrets being so rude to you that first time you were here. When all I wanted was to possess your body and soul – neither of which I deserve. I need to expunge it from your memory and mine. This is different. This time, it's about you. I want to show you how much I treasure you and make amends for not considering your desires. I want you to –" he swallowed, certain she was going to refuse his outrageous request, trying to find words that wouldn't sound as crass as the ones in his head "– lie down on my desk and let me fall to my knees and worship you." He regretted his words as soon as they were out.

Mel backed away, shaking her head, and his heart plummeted. "No, Luce. Angels aren't to be worshipped. We're here to help, not pose as deities."

Luce burst out laughing. "You've got me tongue-tied so I can't say anything right. That's not what I meant. I'm trying to say I want to pleasure your body with mine, here on the desk. My mouth, my hands, my everything – focussed purely on your pleasure. Part of my…penance to you, for being such a prick."

She softened and stepped forward. Her lips tasted of sweet victory as she kissed him, and she didn't resist as he lifted her to perch on the edge of his desk. Luce's eyes didn't leave hers as he shrugged out of his jacket and folded it into a pillow. He tilted her back, so that her head rested on his coat. He dropped to his knees. "Please, Melody," he begged.

Her knees, so modestly pressed together, parted slightly to reveal a glimpse of the soft, white lace underwear that clung to her skin under her skirt. She sighed. "All right, my love."

Five

Luce felt her body shudder in pleasure. Her tiny gasp was all the sound she made. He was losing his touch – she didn't respond to him like other girls did. He'd done his best but he couldn't seem to coax the sort of climax out of her that made her scream his name. He sank to the floor, sitting back on his heels. "I'm sorry, Mel," he said quietly.

He rose, placed her underwear on the desk beside her and dragged himself to the private bathroom adjoining his office. He freshened up, taking unusual care washing his hands to delay the moment when he'd be forced to face her pity for his failure. Eventually, he returned to the office. Luce slumped in his desk chair, watching Mel smooth her skirt down as if she'd experienced no passion at all. She probably hadn't, he told himself.

Mel leaned against the desk and folded her arms. "What are you sorry for, Luce?"

"I can't satisfy you properly. You barely made a sound. Other girls lose control and you…I couldn't…" He closed his eyes, not wanting her to see his anguish. He was a failure – might as well be impotent, if he couldn't satisfy her. She'd leave him and find some angel who could.

Her gentle laughter only made him feel worse. Then her weight settled across his lap, her backside resting on his thighs as her legs pushed his arm off the armrest. "You're sorry because I'm not like other girls? Girls you've corrupted, in other words." Luce stared at her, his guilt rising. "You want to know what I felt while you…while you…" She blushed.

"Yes," he breathed. "I want to know what

I'm doing wrong so I can please you better. I need to know."

Mel cupped his face between her hands and kissed him. The memory she gave him coalesced in his mind, intensifying as her kiss deepened. He felt every stroke of his tongue as though he controlled her body and not his own, on the receiving end of what felt like…

"Oh my God!" Then he couldn't breathe. He couldn't see. He couldn't move and he was about to need clean underwear.

Sensation ebbed before he exploded in his pants – but it'd been damn close. He was shaking from the adrenaline and he wasn't sure he could speak yet.

Mel kissed him again gently. "You are the best I've ever had. I've told you this before. Here, feel my heartbeat – it's racing at just the memory." She slid Luce's hand under her shirt so that he could press his fingers to her breast, over her galloping pulse. Another kiss quickened the beat further.

Luce grinned. His unoccupied hand crept toward her skirt in the hope that she'd let him monitor her heartbeat while he pleasured her one more time. Oh, please…

The office door flew open, framing Mephi in the doorway. Her jaw dropped, but her recovery was rapid. "Mel? Ohhh, I told him he couldn't seduce the staff here. I'll call security and have them throw him out."

Luce returned his wandering hand to the desk, hoping Mephi hadn't seen how close it had been to Mel's thigh.

Mel gently broke their kiss and glanced at Mephi. "No, security won't be necessary. Unless….well, in truth, I jumped Luce, so he's the one who might want security to come and escort me out."

"He has his hand up your shirt," Mephi snapped, her eyes flashing red as she glared at Luce.

Luce tried to shift his hand without Mephi noticing, but Mel placed her hand on her shirt, over her heart and Luce's hand, pressing his fingers against her soft flesh.

"Yes, he does," Mel said, smiling. "But —" she slid out of his lap and moved just out of reach "— from what I understand of the situation here, there will be a lot of work for us to do and it's best that we get started as soon as possible. Later, Luce." She winked.

Mephi's disapproving mouth twitched as if she wanted to smile, but she didn't. Luce had seen her smile before, but she didn't do it very often. Was she really so happy to see him back? Persephone must have made a pretty useless CEO if that was the case. He'd need Mel more than ever – thank God she was working for him and not Lili this time.

Luce cleared his throat. "Ah, Mephi, Mel will be taking on a special projects role for me here and she'll need an office close to mine. Maybe the CFO office? It's not like we can trust any demon to do that job, so it's been empty since I fired Baraqiel."

Mephi's frown deepened. "Miss Angel's desk is still available. It might be best if she returned to it." She gave Mel a meaningful glance that made Luce's jaw drop. He picked it up quickly, hoping she hadn't noticed, as he turned over the possibility in his head that Mephi liked Mel.

Having to cross the whole office to that tiny, cramped cubicle to find Mel? Hell, no!

"Mel won't be doing her old job and she'll need a bigger office. She'll also need a PA. Mephi, can you arrange it? I remember there used to be plenty of office girls running around the place. Surely you can spare one for Mel."

"I really don't need one, Luce," Mel objected. "I've always handled my own schedule and calls. I'm sure anyone you assign to me will get bored with nothing to do."

"If the duties really are as light as you say, I'm sure I can take care of Miss Angel better than anyone else, Mr Iblis. If that's acceptable to you, Me – Miss Angel," Mephi corrected herself.

Mel smiled. "That would be wonderful. Thank you, Mephi. But you know you can call me Mel."

Mephi nodded.

Luce clapped his hands. "That's settled, then. Mephi, call IT and get them to set up the CFO office for Mel. Then alert all staff that they're required for a briefing in the lecture theatre at ten."

The moment the door clicked shut behind

Mephi, Mel said, "Before we were interrupted, I was going to say that if you like, the next time we make love, I'll show you how one of the Hashmallim can manage to withstand even your mindblowing sex without being corrupted."

Like he'd ever refuse her. "You think I'm really that good?"

She laughed. "Yes, my love. You're one sexy devil and you're better than good."

Six

"Once everyone's here, I'll brief them on the change of management and your role here, then let you speak to them," Luce said as they entered the empty lecture theatre. Some idiot had stopped ordering coffee beans for the magnificent coffee machine Mel had won for them, so there was only that instant stuff that he wouldn't touch. He'd sent Mephi out for coffee for Mel and himself. Mel had laughed and said her first task would be to get the espresso flowing again and he couldn't express his appreciation emphatically enough. Maybe after work…

Mel laughed shakily. "Me? Speak in front of everyone? Oh, Luce, that's not a good idea."

"They all know you and they all owe you, too. They'll shut up and listen to you, I swear." The gentle shake of her head brought him up short. "What?"

"Luce, I'm terrified of public speaking. You rescued me from it yourself once in this very room, when the fear overcame me and I fell to my knees. Your kindness that day always stands out in my mind. The room was full of human reporters, yet it was you, a demon, who came to my aid and helped me up." She blushed. "I thought then that you wanted something and you'd use my weakness against me, but you never did."

How could he have forgotten? She'd fallen and the only thought in his head was the irresistible urge to help her. The moment he'd touched her, he'd felt an alien ardour to hold her forever and a powerful yearning for salvation only she could deliver. With his mind scrambling to understand the churning desires, he'd named her his saviour in front of the assembled press. Luckily for him, they'd lapped it up. Or was it Mel's luck that had done it?

"I'll be there, right beside you," he said. "And it's not public speaking when you know them all and they know you. It's like a conversation with a lot of people, all at the same time. Just say that the first thing you're going to do is sort out the coffee situation. Everyone will smile and clap, I'll warn them again not to ask you to unjam the photocopier or they'll be headed straight back to Hell, and we'll end the briefing. You're the most powerful angel any of them have ever seen — capable of obliterating the lot of them if the mood takes you. You have nothing to be afraid of. It'll be fine."

Her nervous smile tugged at his heart. "All right, I'll try." Her pale purple skirt swirled around her legs as she crossed to a chair in the front row and gracefully lowered herself onto it. She made the worn cloth seat look like a throne, though it was no different to any of the others. Every movement she made screamed out that she was no ordinary angel.

How could he have been so oblivious to it before?

At ten, not a second before, demons started trooping in, in groups of two or three. They filled up the middle and rear seats of the lecture theatre, row upon row of dark shirts and suits that made Mel and her pastels stand out all the more. There wasn't even a hint of red among them – Lili must still be in Hell, Luce figured, which was fine by him. His chest still itched at the feel of her claws digging into his heart. He waited, letting them talk among themselves, until Mephi appeared in the doorway and gave a sharp nod. She perched on the edge of the seat nearest the door.

"Good morning," Luce began with a grin. "As you can see, I'm back at the helm of the HELL Corporation and the future's looking brighter than ever. Through my skills of persuasion, Miss Melody Angel has returned as Special Projects Director and, with her assistance, business here in HELL will be better than ever. So I'd like everyone to warmly welcome back…Mel!" Luce waved his arms with a flourish. "Come up here where everyone can see you, Mel."

She gave a painful smile and rose shakily to her feet. When the smattering of applause started, she stumbled, but righted herself before she fell. Her gaze locked on Luce's and he couldn't help but see the determination that drove her to keep walking. Every step seemed to take more willpower than he'd ever owned.

No. He'd promised to stand beside her and he would. Starting now. Luce strode to meet her, wrapping an arm securely around Mel's waist and walking with her the last few steps to the lectern. He was supporting most of her weight by the time he reached it – her legs seemed to want to fold up beneath her – but he couldn't let her fall. Couldn't let her show weakness in front of demons because they'd swarm like seagulls.

They both turned to face the crowd and the clapping abruptly ceased. Mel's hand seized his and he was swamped by a flood of terror so intense he'd never experienced anything like it before. Not his – hers, as her throat froze so she could barely draw breath, let alone speak. Not only did he have to keep her upright, he'd have to speak for his usually eloquent angel.

"Mel and I will be working very closely together for the foreseeable future, so I don't want to hear about anyone asking her to help them out on any project that hasn't been personally approved by me. If you need an appointment with Mel, Mephi will be handling her schedule. And if I hear anyone asking her to do anything with the photocopier, I will personally see that person transferred to Level Eight, effective immediately," Luce thundered.

"Mel, will you be the first point of contact for animal welfare and alien invasion issues?" someone called from the audience.

Luce waited, but Mel still couldn't seem to loosen her tongue, so he answered, "No, you'll refer those matters to whoever has been handling them since she left. Mephi will be screening all her calls, so if you try to call her for anything that I haven't approved –"

"Let her speak for herself!" someone shouted.

"Yeah, let her go!"

Before Luce could work out who had shouted, more than half the demons erupted out of their seats with similar angry shouts. It was like being back in his office in Hell, where every demon had wanted to defend her and beg for her release. Instead of individual demands, though, now there was a demonic cacophony that drowned out the whimpers he could feel escaping from Mel.

"Get out!" he roared over them. "This briefing is over. Get back to work!"

He repeated it several times until all the demons left the lecture theatre. Mephi, who was the last, gave him a dark look as she descended the steps.

"Is Miss Angel all right? What can I do to assist?" Mephi asked, sounding concerned even as her eyes burned red.

"She's fine," Luce said curtly. "You get back to work, too."

He watched as she slowly made her way up the stairs and out the door. It wasn't until they were alone that he pulled Mel into his arms and whispered, "I'm so sorry. I didn't realise it would be this bad."

Mel pushed herself far enough away to look up at him. "The last time I managed to deliver a speech in front of a crowd, they turned into a mob and tore my body to pieces. Thousands of years may have passed, but I can still feel those clawing nails as if it was yesterday. I am…a poor presenter at best, Luce. I'm sorry."

"It's hardly your fault. I won't make you do that again – ever. I swear." He wet his lips. "How can I make it up to you?"

Mel smiled wanly. "Maybe it'd be best if I went outside and got some fresh air for an hour or so before I return to work. I need to pick up a few things, anyway. I'll return in time for lunch."

"Do you want me to come with you to make sure you're okay? I mean, you almost collapsed in here."

She shook her head. "I'll be all right. See you in an hour or so, my love. Don't burn the office down while I'm gone."

Seven

Mel set the bags on her desk, peeping at some of the satin and lace she'd bought when she'd given in to temptation. It wasn't for her, after all…well, it was, seeing as she, and not Luce, would be wearing all that lovely lingerie, but he was the reason she'd bought it. The poor man had cried over her bloodstained bra in Hell, for goodness' sake. He deserved to see her in its replacement. In all of the replacements.

She wanted each item and ensemble to be a surprise, so she opened the desk drawer, hoping to stash them away before he saw them. The drawer was full of bits of paper. Mel pulled one out and squinted at it. A lottery ticket. They were all lottery tickets. She pulled the whole drawer out and emptied the contents on her desk. How many tickets were there? Hundreds, maybe. A closer look revealed that they were more than a year out of date. Even if they'd been jackpot winners, they were null and void now. She transferred the mess to her wastepaper basket and tucked her purchases into her now empty drawer.

Not a moment too soon, either.

A knock at the open door made her look up. Expecting Luce, Mel was surprised to see Nybbas.

He grinned nervously. "Hi, Mel. It's good to have you back. A bit of a promotion for you, isn't it?"

Nybbas was the only person in the whole corporation who could give a worse presentation than her – at least, he had been, until she'd helped him. Mel had always suspected Nybbas had feelings for her, but he'd never dared to go against Luce.

"Perhaps," she said. "It's certainly an improvement to doing Lili's stapling and photocopying." She nodded at her computer. "Are you here to set that up for me?"

He reddened. "No, the imps took care of that this morning while we were in Luce…Lord Lucifer's briefing. I wanted to ask if everything was all right." He sidled into the room, glancing around as if he was afraid to be seen talking to her.

"Why wouldn't it be?" she asked.

He coughed. "Well, Spike – one of the imps – said that he'd seen you in Hell. That Lord Lucifer had you in his lair in the lowest levels. You…you can't trust the imps, you know, because they like to cause trouble. It's what they live for. And demons…well, we can lie like humans. I guess you already knew that. Or I hope you did. But you…you're still an angel, right? And angels can't lie. So I thought if I asked you, at least I'd know it was the truth. Did Lord Lucifer…did he…"

Mel nodded once. "I've seen his lair in Hell, yes. He keeps a two-pronged fork in an umbrella stand behind his desk. A bident, I believe it's called."

Nybbas paled. "You mean it's true? You really are working with Lord Lucifer now?"

She forced herself to smile. "Yes, I'm here to help Luce. I'm sure he explained that in the briefing."

His eyes darted around the room and then to the door before he crept toward her desk. Dropping his voice so low it was barely audible, Nybbas said, "You looked terrified when he touched you this morning, Mel. We've been talking around the office and we think he's gone too far. Corrupting humans and the occasional angel, fair enough, but you –" He swallowed. "If you need help with anything, and I mean anything, tell me. I'd defy Lord Lucifer for you."

"Are you ready for lunch, Mel?" A grinning Luce stood in the doorway, raising his eyebrows suggestively. "I booked us a table at the Hilton's restaurant and the chef tells me he has fresh oysters that just arrived. Don't think you'll get out of it that easily. After what you said this morning…"

Nybbas looked horrified.

Mel blushed. "Yes." She rose and headed for the door. "Thanks for setting up my computer, Nybbas. I'll let you know if I have any trouble with it."

Luce held out his hand and she took it. Together, they made their way to the lift. It looked like everyone was headed out for lunch at the same time, because it seemed to take forever for the lift to reach their floor and the smells wafting up from the atrium lobby were all from food.

Mel inhaled deeply. "I swear I can smell peppermint. Do you think someone spilled peppermint oil in the water feature? We'll be smelling it for days if they have."

Luce sniffed. "Is that what that stench is? Hell, I hope not. I'll talk to building management and make them pump out the whole damn fountain. I won't be able to smell your perfume if my sinuses are stuffed with that!"

Mel laughed softly all the way down to the lobby and out to the arcade. The smell didn't fade as they walked – in fact, it seemed to strengthen until Mel thought she could taste it.

Sugary, sweet and sharp, it was like…

"We have a candy shop here? In the HELL Corporation building? The tenant manager must hate me. Or maybe Persephone approved it. That must be it. Something so sickly sweet has no place in HELL," Luce muttered, glaring at the shop where peppermint rock candy was being made.

Mel stopped and addressed the shop assistant. "My friend isn't a fan of peppermint. Too sweet, he says. Do you have anything a little more sour for him?"

The girl set down her spatula and peeled off her gloves. "How sour do you need it? Dissolve-his-tastebuds-and make-him-pucker-up sour, or the type of tart sweetness that just sort of tingles a bit?"

Squeezing Luce's hand, Mel replied, "I think I can get him to pucker up without dissolving his tongue. I'll take the tingles, please." She laughed with the shop assistant as she paid for a small jar of lemon lollies and presented them to Luce. "Here you go, my love. Something as sour as you want to be."

For a moment, he fought to keep his frown

but it was a losing battle. He burst out laughing and tucked the jar into her bag. "There's lemon in your perfume, isn't there?"

"Lemon blossom, yes."

He stopped laughing, but a rueful smile remained. "I'll share them with you later."

Eight

When Mel returned to her office, there was a note on the computer keyboard:

If you need anything, anything at all, call me – Nybbas.

Beneath the scrawled letters were his extension number and a mobile phone number, too. Mel flipped the note over and tossed it into her empty in-tray. Time to get some work done. She switched on her computer and reached into the top drawer for a pen and something to write on.

Nothing. The bottom drawer now held her lingerie, but the top one was empty. So was the one in the middle. It seemed that the desk had been ransacked during the guerrilla stationery wars in her first contract here and nothing had been replaced. At least she knew where the stationery storeroom was — surely there'd be supplies in it by now.

Mel pushed open the door to the storeroom to find it occupied by an unusually thin man. The only sign of stationery was the cup of pens on the desk, beside his bony elbow.

"Oh, excuse me," she said, backing out. "I thought this was where the stationery was kept. I must have made a mistake."

"Honoured by Lady's visit," the man replied, twisting out of his seat. Short and skinny, he barely came to Mel's shoulder. His protruding eyes seemed huge in his emaciated face. His mouth didn't move as he continued, "How can Sptlk serve Lady?"

She laughed and blinked away the illusion. Sptlk the imp stood on the desk, not the carpet, and the malnourished man didn't exist at all. "You're looking very fit," she said, nodding at his flat belly, which she remembered being a lot rounder.

Sptlk made a disgusted noise in his throat. His voice sounded in her head: "Demonic cost-cutting. No chips and less staff. Agreement with Lord makes imps stay. Payment will be exacted." Images spun rapidly in his thoughts as he showed Mel what had happened in the HELL Corporation offices while she'd been in Hell.

The imps were on the brink of mutiny. They hadn't been paid – in Lucifer's unconventional terms, or in monetary ones – since Luce had left. Beelzebub had sent staff in increasing numbers back to Hell. Staff were required to buy their own stationery if they wanted it – and their own padlocks to keep it from being stolen by the other demons. The last chip Sptlk had eaten had been at Mel's farewell morning tea – until he'd decided to create the illusion of a starving human. With the illusion, an hour's begging at lunchtime yielded him enough money to feed himself and the other imps.

"I'll fix this, Sptlk," Mel vowed. "So, I take it I'm not going to find any stationery in the office? I'll need to get my own?"

Sptlk hesitantly answered in the affirmative.

Mel lifted her chin. "To Hell with that. I'll get Luce to make me the new CFO. I'm in the right office already. All cost-cutting measures will need my approval and I'll be damned before I let this sort of stupidity continue. Tell me: was it Beelzebub or Persephone who made things like this?"

"Demon ordered. Nephilim did nothing. Plays and giggles only. Business trips to Hell."

"Do you know where Persi went? Or why?" Mel figured it was a faint hope, but one worth investigating.

"Nephilim never saw imps nor spoke. Too busy with fallen angel twins." Sptlk's amusement coloured the images of Persi cavorting with Samael and Camael in Luce's office.

Mel held up her hands. "Stop."

"Apologies, Lady." The images vanished and the memory faded a little in her mind. Nowhere near as much as she'd like, though.

"How can Sptlk make amends for forgetting Lady's distaste for lust?"

Mel laughed. "Not all lust. Just the hedonistic sort and watching it in graphic detail. After all, I manage to satisfy Luce just fine and that's probably a miracle in itself."

"No miracle. Lord fortunate having Lady's attention."

Mel caught the edge in the imp's tone, revealing more than Sptlk had perhaps intended. Cautiously, she probed his thoughts and sorrow tinged her own tone as she said, "I'm sorry, Sptlk. I had no idea."

Sptlk laughed bitterly. "Lady loved by many, yet chooses Lord. Lucky Lord. Yet love remains and loyalty. Honoured to be at Lady's service in anything."

"The honour is mine," Mel responded. "And I hope never to ask too much of you. But any work you do for the HELL Corporation must be paid for as if you were any other employee. I'll see to it. And I recommend you move out of this storeroom because I'm going to fix the stationery situation, too. Thanks, Sptlk. Oh, have you had lunch today?"

The imp shook his head.

"Go to Mephi's desk and tell her I authorised your use of her corporate credit card for a catering order. Head downstairs and make sure you get plenty for everyone." Mel winked. "I'll tell her on my way back to my desk."

"Working with Lady pleasure indeed." Sptlk grinned.

That's what Luce had said, too. Mel hid her smile and headed back to her office. She had a whole mess of problems to sort out before the afternoon was over.

Nine

"Someone's violated a directive and there'll be Hell to pay!" a male voice shouted.

Luce rubbed his temples, hoping to ease the building headache. He'd had enough of work to last him all week. From what he'd discovered, he suspected Persephone hadn't done a single work-related thing in his absence. Heaven only knew what she had done, in between her jaunts to Hell to taunt him.

"This'll blow our budget by thousands of dollars this month alone! I won't answer for it!" the voice continued.

Luce gave up and pulled on his jacket. He wanted to lose himself in Mel's arms and forget everything but the bliss he found there.

"Lord Lucifer, it's not my fault!" The voice soared up an octave as the demon who owned it dropped to his knees. Turiel, who dealt with intellectual property and copyright law.

Luce snorted. He was certain he'd made the right decision on Turiel's appointment. After all, who knew better than the demon who'd made copyright infringement an art back in the 1950s? He'd even called the bloody thing a grimoire, as if the obsolete word would give his bastardised book the legitimacy it lacked.

"Who'd you copy this time, then?" Luce asked with a chuckle.

Turiel shook a sheaf of papers so hard they rustled like the maple leaves in the autumn wind outside. "I did nothing! Someone's ordered so much stationery we don't have anywhere to put it! I checked at the delivery centre and the order definitely came from inside HELL. When I find out who placed this order, I'm going to…"

Luce waited, but Turiel seemed to be all out of consequences. And complete sentences. "Kiss them? Make them a bouquet of fresh-sharpened pencils?"

"More like stab them with pencils," Turiel muttered.

Mel appeared in the doorway, her beaming smile and shining eyes claiming Luce's attention. "Pencils? Ooh, have they arrived already? I was hoping I'd have some stationery before I left today. I know I can make notes on my computer, but there's nothing like the feeling of writing task lists by hand and crossing them out when they're complete."

"She did it!" Turiel whined, pointing.

Ignoring the demon, Luce asked, "So what miracles have you worked today?"

Mel lowered her gaze. "Not many. Coffee beans will arrive in the morning because the warehouse was closed by the time I got hold of the delivery rep. Stationery was an easy online order. I found some of the old orders in the previous CFO's files, so I put in an order for what I estimate is about three months' worth — enough to make up the shortfall from no one having ordered any. Nobody's paid the imps, so I made arrangements with HR and payroll, which includes back pay, and I've allocated them a catering budget again. Luce, the company can't operate without a Chief Financial Officer. Hell, I can't even find records of an accountant here. All your financials are a mess."

Luce shrugged. "All in a day's work for an angel. I think you've done enough for today – time to head home for dinner."

"What about punishing her for the stationery?" Turiel demanded.

Punishing Mel for ordering pencils? Luce stared at the demon. "And why should I do that?" He kept his voice calm, but the dangerous undercurrent wasn't far from the surface.

"Because it's not my fault!" he bleated.

"Are you the supply and contracts officer?" Mel asked. "Um, I couldn't find a name on any of the invoices. Just your job title."

"I'm Turiel, and yes, I'm the supply and contracts officer," he snapped. "If you want to purchase something, you need my approval first, so we don't blow the budgets!"

"What budgets?" Mel asked bluntly. "No one's set one for anything this financial year. A lot of big, fat zeroes are all I saw in the accounts spreadsheets."

"Those are the budgets!" Turiel insisted. "And you've just blown them, stupid angel. What do you think Lord Lucifer's going to do to you for that?"

Luce saw red. "Go to Hell. No one insults Mel in front of me."

Turiel's eyes widened in fright before he disappeared, leaving behind a smoking pair of shoes.

Luce dusted off his hands. "Sorry about that, Mel. I'll make sure Mephi sends out a memo to all staff, reminding them not to question you. I wondered why we had no pens left. What kind of stupid idea is it to try and run an office without stationery? It beggars belief. And I think I'd like to take my new CFO out to dinner, if you're willing."

Mel sighed. "Well, I already have the office and I don't think the previous one did much anyway. But dinner will have to wait until after we've been to Persi's place."

"Persi's place?" Luce repeated as his heart turned to ice. Not the nephilim.

"The penthouse that used to be yours. And now I've just looked through all of HELL's financials, it appears it's yours again. The penthouse belongs to HELL as the CEO's official residence. So if you're the CEO, it reverts back to you. But I want to search it for Persi, or clues to where she might be."

"And if we don't find her?"

Mel smiled. "Then you can move back in at your leisure."

"Tonight," he replied instantly. "We can have dinner at the Old Brewery Restaurant, and afterwards we can make love in my bed until dawn. Then we'll watch the dolphins playing in Matilda Bay."

"An ambitious plan," Mel said with a smile. "We'll see. First things first – we search for Persi."

Ten

Luce turned the key, pushed open the door and moved aside to let Mel enter the penthouse first. Some might call him a coward, but Luce didn't much care. He didn't want to be the first person to encounter Persephone in his old apartment. Mel could handle the girl far better than he could, and Persephone wouldn't be hostile to Mel. At least, he hoped not.

"Persi, honey?" Mel called. "It's me, Mel. Just coming to check on you because no one's seen you for a while and you had us all worried. Persi?" She wandered through the apartment, calling the girl's name, but she got no answer. "Luce, can you check the living areas? I'll do the bedrooms and bathrooms."

Luce nodded and peered under the dining table. Nope, no nephilim. Maybe in the lounge.

How well did Mel know Persephone? Luce wondered as he heard the angel's gentle tone calling for her cousin again. Surely she couldn't know everything about her. Not the kinky, sadistic stuff the girl was into, surely. Mel hadn't even agreed to do anything with him when a simple pair of handcuffs were involved.

Luce headed for the kitchen. A quick search of the cupboards revealed nothing unusual. Even the pantry looked just as he'd left it. Had she even lived here at all?

He opened the cupboard behind the bar, where he used to keep his best whiskies, and met the eerie sight of dozens of glittering eyes. Clicking on the light, he breathed a sigh of relief and felt his pumping heart relax as he realised the eyes belonged to an army of china dolls. Some of them showed their age with yellowing lace and cracked varnish on their faces, while others were so glossy and pale they looked brand new. Every single one of them looked like a corpse – the blank faces anything but lifelike. The crazy nephilim had turned his liquor cabinet into a mausoleum.

"Hey, Mel!" he called.

"Mmm?" Her hand touched his back before her fingers began kneading out the tension across his shoulders. "There's nothing to be afraid of here, Luce. I won't let her hurt you."

He snorted, but he knew he couldn't fool her. His locked-up shoulder muscles gave him away. "What's with the weird dolls? Does she have a fetish with death?"

"With death? Why do you say that?" Mel's fingers dug deeper, ironing out all the stress of the day.

Her fingers were magic. Nothing short of miraculous. "The dolls look like dead children. The tattoo she had on her nether regions is a copy of Renaissance artwork depicting the netherworld. The way she always wore black, the same colour as her hair. And how she visited me in Hell, even my lair, when no one else could get in. Well, except you, of course, but I'd never want to keep you out. Just everyone else." He moaned softly.

"Well, there was that unfortunate incident when she was very young. Hades kidnapped her and dragged her into the Underworld for a time. It was very traumatic for her and I'm sure there were lasting effects on her psyche. If my terror at public speaking has lasted this long…" Mel laughed shakily. "Well, Persi might be afraid of death, and this is how she deals with it. Maybe her coping strategy is more effective than mine. When we find her, I must ask her."

"She's not here, is she?" Luce asked.

Mel shook her head. "The place looks exactly the same as we left it, when we came to collect your things."

"So she's been missing since then?" Even as he said it, he knew it couldn't be true. Persephone hadn't been missing when she was harassing him in Hell. She'd gone missing while he and Mel were in Heaven. He wondered if it was because she was jealous of Mel.

"There should be dust, but there's none. That means she must have been here less than a week ago, surely."

Luce hesitated, but knew he'd have to say it. "I have a cleaner. Someone who comes and cleans the place once a week, every Friday. I had an email from her saying her invoices hadn't been paid, so I fixed that today. She was here last Friday…or at least she said she was and I paid her for it. If the place isn't dusty, it's because of the cleaner." His brain kicked into gear. "Wait. If Persephone's been here since Friday, the beds will be made differently. She always does them like hospital beds."

Luce hurried to his old bedroom, the one with the incredible view he wanted Mel to wake up to. He ran his hand down the corners of his bed and relaxed a little more. "Your cousin didn't make this bed. The sheets were fresh on Friday and haven't been touched since. I'll check the guest beds, too." The other two beds yielded the same result: no sign of Persephone having slept in them. A swift check through the walk-in wardrobes revealed a few items of women's clothing, a huge collection of shoes and many empty spots where things were missing. Her suitcase was nowhere to be found, either. He returned to the lounge to report this to Mel. "So she must be travelling somewhere," he concluded, settling onto the three-seater.

Mel sank onto the seat beside him. "Her favourite sex toys are gone. All of them. That means she intended to travel for some time."

Luce shot upright. "You know about those?"

Mel laughed softly. "I'm hardly innocent, Luce. Just because I've never used them, doesn't mean I'm ignorant of their form or function. I could say the same about certain parts of your anatomy, too."

To his own surprise, Luce blushed.

"Let me show you," he suggested, hearing the lust in his voice but not caring. Mel could handle him. Or not, as she desired.

She pushed him away and rose. "After dinner. We have to head back to my place to pick up some clothes and stuff for tomorrow, then I'd like to eat. I'm willing to bet you know a place nearby that serves oysters, just the way you like them."

He laughed. "Sure do. Are you saying I'll need them?"

Mel wet her lips. "Perhaps."

Eleven

"That was exactly what I needed after today. The office really is Hell. I've never worked a day as bad as that before." Luce pressed his lips to Mel's breast, rejoicing in the rapidity of her heartbeat. At least he could do something right. "It's the first time I've ever been happy I signed over the whole damn corporation to someone else."

Mel released a deep sigh. "I'm sorry, Luce. You shouldn't have to deal with it any more. Persi and HELL aren't really your problem. I just thought the demons would respond better to you than they would to me. I never thought…"

Luce chuckled. "They're demons. A pack of brawling cats is easier to control. Yet you seem to unite them in ways I wouldn't have believed possible if I didn't know you. I didn't realise that I wasn't the only demon who fell for you when you worked in my office before. I'm lucky you decided to be my angel and not someone else's." Or he'd have had to slaughter the other demons daily until the dopey bastards got the message that no one took Melody from the Lord of Hell. Damn demons, couldn't even kill them properly, what with them healing back to normal overnight.

"They're still not your problem any more. I wanted your help in HELL because you're the CEO they know and recognise, the one they're used to obeying. But if you really don't want to do it, it's fine. I should have asked what you wanted before dragging you back into HELL. I guess I'll just have to do it myself. I'll go into the office tomorrow and tell Mephi –"

"That you're Melody Angel, CEO of HELL

Corporation? While I…what? Stay here and bake biscuits for you?" Luce snorted. Mel didn't want to be the CEO any more than he did and he could hear it loud and clear in her voice.

"Well, if you're offering, I am partial to choc chip ones and butter shortbread…and chocolate brownies, if your baking talents run to cakes, too." Mel burst out laughing when Luce's startled eyes met hers. "I was joking, my love. Well, not about what I like, but I'd never ask you to stay home and cook while I go to work. Despite what I said to Raphael, you're under no obligation to help. You can spend all day sailing or lying on the beach or feeding swans, if you wish. After today, they all know I'm at HELL with your approval. I'm sure I can maintain the corporation without your presence."

"After seeing what one attempt at public speaking did to you? Not a hope in Hell, Melody. Demons may be difficult to deal with, but they're as much my problem as yours." Luce pulled her close and held her tight. "There's no way in Hell I'll sit around and do nothing while you're slogging your guts out in my company, even if it isn't mine any more. If you're there, I will be, too."

He felt her body relax, even as her arms tightened around him. "Thank you," she said, her voice muffled by his muscles. Not that he was complaining about her lips tickling his nipples. "You have no idea how happy it makes me to hear you say that. I can't imagine HELL without you and I'm not sure I'd want to. No one deals with demons quite the way you can."

"I'd like to think that I'm good at more than just demon-wrangling," Luce replied. "And with two of us, we'll share the workload so that I can take you out to coffee, to lunch, and maybe schedule some one-on-one meetings where we lock the office door and I can show you all of my talents." He grinned at the ceiling. "You'll have to wear a skirt to work every day."

Mel slid out of bed and reached for her nightgown, letting the pale gold satin caress her curves as it slid over her skin. "It all sounds lovely," she said carefully, "but I don't think we should have too many afternoon meetings. While you're definitely a very sexy devil, my love, that desk is hard and uncomfortable. I prefer the bed here." She perched on the edge and patted the firm mattress.

"Better than the one in your house, definitely," Luce replied. "So we're staying here because it's closer to the office and has a better bed?"

Mel looked like she was trying to hold back laughter. "Yes, we'll stay here, but because Persi might turn up here. I admit I won't miss squeezing into sardine trains to get to work — the morning walk along the river instead will be wonderful." Her loving smile set his heart alight. "Especially with you."

Twelve

Sarkis entered through the open door. There was no need to knock – he was expected. Summoned, even.

"Sir?" he asked, fixing his gaze on his superior. Both plain men used to the campaign life of Roman soldiers, even now as angels they shared the same taste in simplicity. A worn table and two chairs were all the furniture in this Heavenly office.

"Sit down, my friend. I have a favour to ask," George said, gesturing to the unoccupied chair.

Sarkis sat. "If you want me to banish Baraqiel back to Hell permanently, I'll do it gladly. He inspires riots like you wouldn't believe. I thought the one in Egypt was bad. This one in the US…if I weren't an angel, I'd bring some serious retribution down on his head. D'you think I can get permission to do some smiting? Just the demon, me and a sword. No humans…"

George chuckled. "No, I'm afraid I have bigger and better things in mind than that fallen nuisancc. But this assignment comes with a strict order that there are to be no swords."

"None? So it can't be anything to do with demons. Sounds like quite a favour, sir," Sarkis drawled, eyeing his superior. They dealt with demons – it was in their job description.

"Oh, there are demons. And a concentration of some pretty senior ones, too, if the rumours are to be believed. Including a shot at Lucifer."

Sarkis straightened. "Lucifer? I'd need a whole squad to take him on. And the rumours

I've heard…" He coughed.

"What rumours?"

"Too ridiculous to be believed. I heard that Lucifer's managed to get back into Heaven and he left Persephone in charge of Hell, which is why demons are wreaking havoc everywhere while Demeter's daughter sleeps her way through the pick of the demonic ranks. I heard it from Baraqiel, so I put it down to him trying to cause trouble by spinning tall tales. I'd have believed it of Lilith, but Persephone? She wants her wings too much for that."

George sighed. "There's some truth in the rumours. Lucifer entered Heaven – I witnessed it myself. Me and a host of other angels. Dark wings, the works – oh, it was definitely him. "

Sarkis' eyes narrowed. "And Michael let it happen? I don't believe it."

"There was an earlier incident with Michael, Demeter and…a sword. An angel blocked the blow and her body perished. So…no Michael and no swords."

"Her?" There were plenty of female angels, but few high enough to issue orders for one of the Exousiai to disarm. Unless it wasn't the angel herself but the target who was important. "You want me to play guardian to a fledgling angel that Lucifer's set his sights on? And she's only agreed to be bait if I go unarmed?" Sarkis snorted. "Going up against Lucifer unarmed. Are you trying to destroy me, sir?"

George seemed to shrink in his seat. "No. You're not on the list. Raphael sent me a list of Exousiai he wants – good men, all of them, but they're all the sort who are good at taking orders, not giving them. I want to send you with them as their commander. I'd go myself but you're the better choice. And…you've worked with her before."

Sarkis shook his head. "I work alone or with a few hand-picked Exousiai. Not neophytes. You're mistaken."

"Raphael said there's the chance of promotion out of it. A chance to become Hashmallim. No more dealing with riots. Just advising leaders. Next time you visit the US, you could be dealing with Barack Obama, not Baraqiel." George swallowed. "I'll never be Hashmallim. But you could be."

Something still smelled fishy. "That's not

Raphael's decision to make. Oh, he can make recommendations, but no one enters the Hashmallim without higher authority than his. And the Melody Angel's as elusive as mist."

"Not if you're her guardian. You and your men."

Not a neophyte but the highest angel on Earth? What in Heaven's name did she need Exousiai for? Sarkis laughed. "Have you met her? She doesn't need a guardian. She can take on Lucifer all on her own."

"Raphael says differently. And the rumours say that she's the angel who perished, which seems to support why he said the disarm order comes from her, but none of the names are men she's worked with before. None of this makes any sense. That's why I need you. You know her and you'll be able to get to the heart of the matter. The others…give them a demon to fight or thwart and they're brilliant. Intrigues and politics…Freyja doesn't choose us for our grasp of governing." George leaned forward and extended his hand. "Please, my friend. I can order you to do it, but I'd prefer you to take the assignment willingly. It's an honour to work with the Melody Angel. Raphael said Lucifer's seducing her to get him reinstated in Heaven. If he gets his position back, all the fallen angels might return. Do you want Baraqiel wreaking havoc in Heaven?"

Sarkis clasped his hand in a warrior grip. "I will do it, but if I see Lucifer, I'm going to take him to task over Baraqiel. I want that pest confined to Hell."

"Thank you, Sarkis. Take your team and make haste. Lucifer isn't one to waste time. Especially when it comes to seducing angels."

Sarkis managed a smile and left George's office. Sure, it was an honour to work with the Melody Angel, but he knew it wasn't an honour the lady wanted to bestow on him. He knew why he wasn't on her list. If only he hadn't called her a whore the moment they met.

Thirteen

"To a successful fortnight in HELL together!" Luce lifted his wine glass and clinked it against Mel's before taking a gulp that dwarfed her careful sip.

Her worried smile set him on edge. It had to mean bad news. Had she found Persephone?

"Luce," Mel said softly. "You remember when we were talking…oh, ages ago, about how sometimes the wrong staff end up assigned to a task even when they're not qualified?" She set her glass down. "I believe it was when I was handling complaints calls on Reception one day and you were kind enough to bring me a coffee."

"You don't like the way I make your coffee?" Luce was stunned. Mel didn't lie and she'd said she liked it. What was he doing wrong?

Mel's warm fingers closed over his. "No, I love it when you make me coffee. It's perfect every time." Her smile held nothing back. "It's not your qualifications I'm questioning. It's every other demon you employ. They're a lazy bunch of bludgers who wouldn't work if you whipped them – unless you're watching. Then they provide a million excuses as to why they can't do their job, or they do it so slowly that the world will end before it's finished."

Luce shrugged. "Well, that's our contract. We're supposed to do the job as well as human civil servants do theirs. I brought in some specialist souls – damned ones who'd been civil servants in the past – and they instructed my staff on the intricacies of government bureaucracy and time-wasting. It's quite an art."

Mel sighed and swallowed her bite of Turkish bread. "You brought in the worst civil servants in history to train your demons? Oh my….Luce, talk about time-wasting. Demons don't need to be trained in how to be lazy. They're experts at it already. Let me bring in some angels. I'm sure a few of the lower-level ones have office experience."

Luce almost choked on his burger. "Angels and demons working together in the HELL Corporation? You'll start the Heavenly Battle all over again — only this time, in the photocopy room! The imps will go on strike in protest if they have to hide fighting angels and demons!"

"We've had angels and demons working together just fine for a long time now. There's Gabi and Persi — they've worked here without any trouble, and you even offered Camael and Samael jobs with you. No one's ever so much as picked a fight with me." She smiled as she took another bite of her lunch.

He stared at her. "Who'd be stupid enough to pick a fight with you? Except maybe…" He trailed off uncertainly as he remembered Mel's odyssey through Hell. "Okay, maybe some demons are that stupid. But we can send those back to Hell very easily. Level Eight always needs more staff. And those two girls had you to smooth the way for them. Gabrielle stayed on Reception and avoided the rest of us because she was afraid she'd be tainted. Persephone…well, she was only here for a day. As for the twin angels…those two were Lili's playmates. Heaven knows what she saw in them."

"If I bring angels in, I'll be here to smooth the way for them, too. And yes, it might be a good idea to separate them from most of the demons to start with. Give them their own unit or department. After a few weeks or months of sharing the coffee machine, maybe I'll try to integrate them into the other units. This would be a lot easier if you just employed normal humans, Luce."

He shook his head violently. "We tried that. Every human who entered HELL was like fresh meat to a pack of hyenas. Some of the demons were placing bets on how long they'd last until they got corrupted. All the office girls joined Ananiel's brothel after they'd…they'd…" He turned red. He couldn't tell her about all the girls he'd had in his office. The last time he'd mentioned them…oh shit, was she reading his mind? His panicked thoughts evaporated as Mel's lips touched his, melting his mind into a melange of fantasies about what he'd like to do to her. On his desk or at home tonight, or even on this table right now…

Mel broke the kiss with a laugh. "You're incorrigible, my love. Yes, we'll need plenty of angels in HELL to protect the human employees from the demon ones. I've already asked Raphael to find me some likely candidates. I gave him a list of names, but there are a lot of other priorities right now, so it might take some time. In the meantime, we should probably get back to work, as there's plenty more to do before we can go home today." She drained her wineglass and dabbed her lips with her serviette. Gracefully, she rose from her seat and waited.

Luce's gaze fixed on a table at the other side of the restaurant and he jumped to his feet. "It appears you have an admirer," he said as his cutlery clattered to his empty plate.

79

Fourteen

Mel wondered if he was joking. "I do?" She followed Luce's gaze to a table of fit-looking men who were engaged in what appeared to be a heated discussion, punctuated with occasional glances in their direction. The exception was one man who seemed intent on staring right at her.

Luce shrugged, as if it was no surprise that other men desired his angel. "Well, if he's thinking about coming over here to ask you out, I'd better show him he's wasting his time."

He pulled her close and delivered a passionate kiss, letting his hands linger on her body as he looked deep into her eyes. "I feel a sudden urge to cancel all my afternoon meetings and spend some very personal time with you, my sweet Melody." Another kiss followed, making Mel blush as she noticed that all of the men were staring at them now.

Recognition flared and a memory surfaced. Gently, she disengaged from Luce. "He's Exousiai! They all are. I didn't realise Raphael had summoned all of them, or that they'd arrived already. I need to speak to them. You enjoy your meetings and I'll see you back at the office later this afternoon." She paused, then added, "And no sending anyone to Level Eight without asking me first! If you keep sending staff back to Hell, no one will have any idea what they're doing, and it takes so long to train new staff. Yes, even if they're not very good at their jobs, that's better than nothing."

A look of mild irritation crossed Luce's face, but it was quickly replaced by one that was far more calculating. "I'll be lenient with the Water Unit boys if you agree to come out to dinner with me tonight. I'd really like some oysters." Mel smothered a laugh and nodded. With one last smouldering look, Luce turned and strode back to the office.

Shaking her head, Mel made her way over to the Exousiai. She singled out the one she'd recognised. "It's Sarkis, isn't it? I haven't seen you since the summer of the rebellion, with all that brutality in Wexford." She extended her hand to the man, who seemed too stunned to respond. After some time, he grasped Mel's fingers and kissed them, which only made her laugh.

"I'm honoured that you remember me after so long. I was sent to help Patrick and I felt like such a failure when he said we'd have to call in an expert to sort out the trouble. When you showed up, Patrick was so excited to see you that I thought you were..." Sarkis coughed, his cheeks turning rosy. "I'm deeply sorry."

Mel laughed merrily. "I'd been in France so long that I kissed Patrick's cheeks without thinking. You almost exploded as you called him and me some names I'd never heard of and blamed all the brutality on him missing his mistress. Poor Patrick was devastated to lose so many souls on both sides of the conflict." She eyed him as she prised her hand from his grasp. "It happens to the best of us. Humans have free will to make the most appalling choices sometimes."

Sarkis seemed to take heart at her words, covering his emotion by ordering his colleagues to get her a chair, a drink and anything else she wanted.

Amid the whirlwind of activity, one man managed to get her attention. "Please excuse me, miss," he began nervously, "but the man you were having lunch with. I'm not sure if you knew, but he looked a lot like Lucifer."

There was a sudden, stunned silence – broken by a half-dozen voices all speaking at once.

"Lord of Hell…"

"Seductive devil…"

"No angel is safe…"

"…drag you down into Hell and corrupt you…"

"Don't fall for his lies!"

"Raphael said we have to protect you, but…"

Sarkis was the only one who remained silent, his eyes intent on Mel.

She held up her hands for quiet. "I understand your concern, especially since he most definitely is Lucifer. He's also my responsibility. Your concern should be the rest of the demons in his corporation. There are plenty of them around and every one of them just loves making life difficult."

"Ma'am, I'm not sure you realise just how seductive the devil can be," a hard-faced man piped up. "He'll persuade you to fall and you'll be powerless to stop him from dragging you down to Hell with him. It's a good thing we're here to protect you. We'll form a security detail immediately to escort you home and arrange a round-the-clock rotation."

Mel's expression hardened, but she forced herself to keep smiling. "I thank you for the sentiment, but I mean what I say. By all means, stay away from Luce if you fear for your soul. Focus on the other demons. As for seductive – I don't think you realise how much I know about him. I've seen his lair in Hell, as well as some of his regular haunts here on Earth. Would you like to know how good he is in bed?" She winked impishly, before continuing in a softer tone, "Lucifer is mine and I don't require your protection. Anyone who comes between us will regret their interference – up to and including Raphael. Instead, I would like your help. Those of you who are willing to help me take over the HELL Corporation from within, meet me in my office on the seventh floor at nine on Monday morning. I'll officially welcome you to HELL."

She rose and met Sarkis' gaze. "I think it might be best if you explain to your colleagues who I am, in order to prevent any future misunderstandings. If you're the staff Raphael summoned here at my request, then you will follow my orders. Or I'll send you back to George and ask for suitable replacements." She inclined her head toward Sarkis. "It was lovely to see you again."

"Yes, ma'am. See you in HELL on Monday morning," he replied firmly.

Mel smiled in response and left the

muttering Exousiai behind. Raphael hadn't passed on vital information to any of them. She needed to correct his oversight as soon as possible.

Fifteen

Mel's phone trilled and she answered it.

"Mel? It's Armaros at Reception. I have some angels to see you. They're refusing to sign in as visitors, though. Something about signing devilish documents."

She smothered a laugh. "Ah, I forgot about that. I'll be right down."

Eight angels stood in a loose defensive formation between the reception desk and the door, warily covering every angle. Settling them down would be a challenge. Luckily, she'd cleared her morning schedule for this.

"Follow me, please," she said, holding the door open.

Armaros cleared his throat and looked pointedly at the visitors book.

Mel summoned a smile. "Not necessary. They're under contract to the agency and they'll be working here on a special project for me. That makes them HELL Corporation staff, not visitors."

She led the way to the boardroom. As she passed various demon colleagues, she wished each one a good morning.

She strode to the projector screen and waited for the last angel to close the door grumpily behind him. Instead of sitting like his colleagues, he straightened, taking up a sentry post beside the door.

"I'd like everyone sitting down, please," Mel said softly.

The sentry hesitated and looked askance at Sarkis, who gave a barely perceptible nod. The sentry hurried to a seat.

It's not public speaking. It's just a small meeting, Mel told herself as she took a deep breath. She could feel her knees weakening already. "Welcome to HELL, a corporation staffed by demons under contract to humans. You'll be working alongside them, in cooperation –"

"When Hell freezes over," one man interrupted, catching her eye.

Sarkis jumped to his feet and the man corrected himself, "When Hell freezes over, ma'am."

Mel burst out laughing. "Have you ever seen Hell? Any of you?" Heads shook slowly. "The lowest level in Hell is frozen over. A series of ice lakes used for both punishment and cooling some of the administration areas of Hell, including Lucifer's private office and apartment. Hell froze over thousands of years ago, so it's not an excuse that'll work here."

Glances were exchanged around the table and Mel felt their unease increase, though it couldn't match hers. The longer this took, the more her knees felt like they were going to buckle.

Sarkis cleared his throat. "Ma'am, there was considerable discussion last night about you,

Lucifer and Lilith. You do look a lot like her and everyone knows no angel's been into Hell and come out untainted, so it's a lot to take in. Especially when we all saw how close you let Lucifer get yesterday. The boys would like some assurances that you're who you say you are. What with the doors closed and all, it's not like there are any demons around to see. We deal with demons every day and the distrust sort of comes with the territory, so to speak."

Mel nodded. She understood. Closing her eyes, she released the restraints on her power, feeling it flow around her as comfortably as it did in Heaven. Her skin tingled as her lavender linen dress transformed into gold silk. The weight of her wings faded into being, heavier than she remembered, as they stretched from ceiling to floor. She permitted the glow to continue haloing her whole body as it would on a formal occasion in Heaven – this was no time for half measures. These angels could handle the radiance of one of their superiors. Heaven knew she needed all the strength she could muster to do this.

The door moved silently open and Luce

sidled in, carrying two cups of coffee. He clicked the door shut behind him and beamed at Mel. "Sorry I'm late. The coffee machine ran out of milk and I had to send Mephi –"

His voice was drowned out by the scrape of eight angelic swords sliding out of their sheaths as the Exousiai moved between Luce and Mel.

Sarkis stood closest to her. "We're here to protect you, ma'am."

Mel sighed. "Not from Luce or my morning coffee. Please put them away, sit down and let me set things straight."

Luce swept past the defensive line and circled the boardroom table until he stood at Mel's side. "I keep my promises," he said, handing over her mug. "And you look heavenly."

She inhaled and brought the macchiato to her lips.

"Ma'am, don't!" Sarkis cried. "You don't know what's in that!"

"Yes she does," Luce responded mildly. "If I've stuffed it up, I'll have to make another cup, and this meeting's running late enough as it is. Now, Mel said to put your swords away and sit down, which sounds like a great idea to me." He enthroned himself in the chair closest to Mel and winked at her over his coffee. "Do you care to wager how long it'll take before they realise they look ridiculous, guarding against an empty threat with weapons so obsolete they belong in a museum? Where did you dig these angels up, Mel? Or are they the best Raphael could find?"

The angels bristled even more, showing no signs of backing down. "We don't take orders from demons," one said, baring his teeth.

Oh Hell. This was harder than she'd imagined. Why couldn't Raphael have briefed them properly so she didn't have to undergo this ordeal? Maybe when she opened her eyes they'd be the friendly angels she was used to and not the cold, hard warriors they turned into in the presence of demons. If only…

Warm fingers enveloped hers and Mel stared down at Luce's reassuring hand. She could do this. She could. And Luce would help her.

She took a deep, calming breath. "Who did

George place in command?"

Sarkis bowed. "That would be me, ma'am."

"Good. Sarkis, get your boys to stand down. I don't have all day for this briefing and I want you settled in by lunch. I'd like you to summarise what you've been told and I'll see what I can do to sort this mess out."

"In front of him?" Sarkis jerked his head at Luce.

Luce grinned and slurped his coffee as he stood. "Paranoid Powers. Excuse me, Exousiai. If it'll make it easier for you, Mel, I'll leave. If their orders come from Raphael, I can imagine what they are anyway. They've been told to watch my every move and protect you from me." He kissed her hand. "I'll be waiting in my office until you want me, Mel. I promised you Japanese for lunch and you know I'll deliver."

Mel's fingers tightened around his. "No, I'd like you to stay, Luce. This is ridiculous and it must stop. Gentlemen, may I introduce Luce Iblis, the CEO of the HELL Corporation and we'll be working in cooperation with him as —"

"We also don't cooperate with demons. We

hunt them down and banish them back to Hell."

Mel wasn't sure which angel had spoken, but she didn't wait to work it out. She continued, "Luce Iblis, also known as Lucifer, Lord of Hell and he's no longer a demon. So any attempt to banish him to Hell won't work." She paused for a moment to let her words sink in. "Sarkis, for everyone here, could you please describe your chain of command, starting with the highest rank?"

Sarkis coughed. "Well, highest is you, ma'am. After that, Raphael, then St George, then me."

She nodded serenely. "And your orders from George are?"

"Come here and find out what in Hell's going on," he replied promptly.

"From Raphael?"

He hesitated. "Protect you. And no swords."

Blades lowered and slid back into sheaths.

Sarkis swallowed. "Your orders, ma'am?"

Mel smiled. "I'd like you to sit down and listen to what I have to say. Afterwards, you can ask all the questions we have time for. And anyone who doesn't feel that they can conscionably follow my orders may leave."

"No, ma'am."

She raised her eyebrows and Sarkis continued, "Yes and no, ma'am. They'll be sitting and listening, but they won't be leaving. In a hostile situation where a squad of us are surrounded by demons, we follow orders under the chain of command. And we don't desert our comrades in arms. Anyone who can't do that has no place in the Exousiai."

Sarkis and the other angels promptly sat down and gave her their full attention. Scrutiny…oh Hell. She squeezed Luce's hand and felt his love and support flow through the connection.

Mel forced herself to say, "I think you'll find the HELL Corporation is less hostile than you expect."

"No, ma'am. We're in the presence of the Lord of Hell, who, demon or not, has every demon on Earth and in Hell under his command. The only thing I trust a demon to do is raise Hell."

Luce burst out laughing. "I've changed my

mind. I like this one." He raised his empty cup to Sarkis.

Sarkis didn't smile.

Mel blew out a breath. "All right. I'd like you boys to form a complaints department here in HELL."

Sarkis looked like he was trying not to laugh, but he managed to compose himself.

She hurried to get the words out before her voice died. "It's not a joke. I'll arrange one of the agency girls to take your calls – Gabi's good with a switchboard, so she'd be my first choice – and your job will be to investigate complaints about anything the HELL Corporation has jurisdiction over. Based on the calls I've fielded, most of them will be from humans, and they'll be human problems for you to investigate and solve within your level of expertise...up to and including working miracles. You'll report direct to me, no one else. Now, if you get a complaint against one or more of the demonic staff here...just like you usually do, I want you to investigate and report back to me on the incident. I'll discuss your preferred course of action with Luce and get back to you on what you're authorised to do."

Mel paused to stare at Sarkis' raised hand. "Yes?"

"I have a question," said Sarkis. "What if the complaint is about a demon inciting city-wide riots? Lots of people injured and lots of property damage…would you consider exile to Hell at sword-point appropriate action?"

"It would depend on the demon and the circumstances, but perhaps –"

"Was it Baraqiel?" Luce interrupted.

Sarkis nodded once.

"Then no. He's supposed to be in Level Eight, serving out a year after his last escape from Hell. Exile's not good enough. This time, I'm going to chain him to something. Several somethings. You do the exile thing and I'll send a note to Geryon to expect him and take care of it when he arrives." He met Mel's stare. "What? I'm still the Lord of Hell. Demons are my problem. I never had the luxury of choosing the perfect person for the job. I make do with those that were dumped in Hell with me. Do you want him in one of the

HELL Corporation units instead? He's not trained for anything except causing trouble. No way in Hell do I want him up here in the office again. He's utterly useless for anything but target practice. If they send him back to Hell in pieces, fine by me. He'll fit in a smaller box."

Mel breathed an inward sigh of relief as the tension in the room broke: most of the angels grinned, or at least looked less grim. Yes, this would work. Thank Heaven Luce was an expert at demon wrangling – he'd been doing it for longer than most of the Exousiai. And there was nothing these soldiers respected more than a veteran.

Sixteen

Mel closed the door to her office and walked right into Luce's welcoming arms. Relief cascaded from her like a warm shower. It was over. The Exousiai complaints unit were in their secluded office space, segregated from demons by virtue of their converted storeroom location.

"You were magnificent, Melody," she heard him say.

Against his chest, she managed a watery smile of disbelief. She'd succeeded, and that was all that mattered. She wasn't sure what she would've done without him there. Who'd have guessed a year ago that she'd be thankful for Lucifer?

"Thank you," she said, her voice muffled by his shirt.

The door clicked open. Mel turned her head to see who'd intruded on what should have been a private moment, but she didn't let go of Luce for fear her wobbly legs would betray her. "Yes?" she asked.

Sarkis squeezed into the room and shut the door behind him. "I didn't want to interrupt, ma'am, but I need to discuss a personal matter."

Mel kissed Luce on the lips before gently disengaging from his embrace. He reminded her to grab him when she wanted lunch, then left her alone with Sarkis, who got straight to the point.

"Ma'am, what were you so afraid of in there?"

Mel sighed. For all of Luce's talk of magnificence, she knew she'd been a nervous wreck.

"Sit down, Sarkis. And please call me Mel. If I let demons do it, you certainly can." She waved at the client chair on the other side of her desk.

"Ma'am…Mel…if you're afraid of Lucifer, you know we're here to protect you. As it is, I don't know how to make head or tails of whatever's going on here. Raphael says one thing, you say another; and while I'd usually say Lucifer is the Lord of Lies, I didn't spot a single untruth today. What's the world coming to when a demon is more honest than an angel?"

"Difficult times, as I'm sure you know," Mel replied. "No, I'm not afraid of Luce. I'm more than a match for him and he's a surprisingly good match for me, though for different reasons. My problem today was…personal and quite embarrassing, really, so I'd prefer not to discuss it. Luce knew I'd struggle today and he was trying to help."

Sarkis nodded. "And what would you do if one of my men had attacked Lucifer – in your defence, of course?"

Mel bit her lip. "As I did before Heaven's

gates, I'd defend him."

"So no swords for any of my men?" He coughed. "That's going to be difficult to enforce, given the number of demons here."

"I don't object to weapons in the slightest, just not in the office. Especially anywhere near Luce." Mel sighed. "Perhaps tell your men that Luce has my permission to insert any weapon used offensively up its owner's fundamental orifice, though I'm sure you'll put it more succinctly than that."

"Attack Lucifer and he'll shove your sword up your arse," Sarkis blurted out, then thought better of it. "Sorry, ma'am. I mean Mel."

She laughed. "Oh, I've heard worse. Wait until you hear the harpies talking about the latest erotica book they're reading in the lunchroom. I'm sure even your boys will blush. I know I do."

"So the official position is what you told us in the café – Lucifer is your responsibility and we're to stick to the lesser demons?"

Mel nodded slowly.

"And what about the unofficial one? What is the Lord of Hell to you?"

While she preferred honesty to lies, some information was not for common knowledge. "Luce and I are together. It's not a secret, but we do try to keep our relationship quiet, as it does shock many people. Of course he's seductive, but he's more than that to me, or his brash brand of seduction would have gotten him nowhere. Despite his dark wings, Luce is no demon – I couldn't have considered what we have if he wasn't an angel. And while he might hide things from others, he can't hide anything from me." At Sarkis' suspicious look, she reached out. "Give me your hand, Sarkis. Let me show you what I mean."

He reluctantly placed his hand on hers. "I'm a soldier, not a soul-reader, so I apologise in advance if I don't understand."

Mel laughed. "It takes a lot of practice and I've had the time for it. You'll see just fine." She closed her eyes and focussed on the memory of the stormy night when Luce came to her home, begging for help and a kiss. She watched the memory fondly until the kiss was complete, then gently pulled her hand from Sarkis'. He didn't need to know how far they'd proceeded after the kiss. "You see?"

Sarkis fell to his knees, his eyes firmly fixed on the carpet. "I'm sorry, my lady. I should never have doubted you. It takes a powerful angel to survive an encounter with Lucifer and before today I'd have said his redemption was impossible. Yet you…you…conquered the darkest demon there is with a simple kiss. I am…in awe."

Mel smiled shyly. "You make it sound like it was all my doing, when Luce's own fortitude played a significant part in his redemption. Without his powerful desire to conquer his own darkness, nothing I did would've helped him at all." She paused for a moment, then continued, "Most demons aren't aware of the change. The very nature of their souls prevents soul-reading. But with Luce on my side, I want to take his initial idea of a global HELL Corporation and turn it into a power for good. While deals and domination are definitely demonic, a company with this sort of worldwide reach can help untold millions. But for that, I need your team to police the demons, to make sure humans don't suffer while the company grows. I need you to maintain order the way only Exousiai can, because I have other responsibilities." She glanced down. "Please get up. I try to keep things very low-key around here as many of the demons have never heard of Lady Muriel, nor the power I hold." She waved at herself and the simple linen dress she wore once more. "No wings, no gold finery, no glow. To them, I'm very much an ordinary angel called Mel."

Sarkis clambered stiffly to his feet. "An extraordinary angel who can do the impossible and negotiate a middle road between angels and demons. Don't doubt yourself. I will do whatever you need me to. What would you like me to report to George?"

"Whatever you feel you need to. I'd recommend full disclosure, as that would make it easier for you to request reinforcements should the need arise. If I know him, he already suspected something when Raphael requested Exousiai to do the work of a lowly guardian angel."

Sarkis executed an elaborate bow. "Being

your guardian would be an honour and nothing less. It's a pity you need no such protection."

This time, they laughed together.

Seventeen

Mephi perched on Luce's visitor chair beside Mel. Luce watched with interest as his PA returned Mel's smile before donning her usual professional mask. The demon dropped a yellow folder on Luce's desk and tapped with a scarlet-lacquered fingernail. "I have everything you asked for, Mr Iblis. Miss Black's schedule, travel arrangements, bookings, credit card statements. I have some of her email and IT records, too."

Luce leaned forward. "I'm sorry. Miss

Black?"

"Persephone Black is the name she goes by at present, Luce," Mel said. She seemed uncomfortable about something, but didn't say anything else.

Mephi's pursed lips expressed her disapproval. "You didn't know your own PA's name?"

"I only met her a few days before we flew out," Luce replied defensively. "She handled all the travel arrangements, not me. And you'd booked everything in my name. I never needed to use her name." He grinned. "All I had to do was snap my fingers and –"

"Mr Iblis, I have explained the concept of sexual harassment to you. Would you like another briefing to refresh your memory?" Mephi's stern expression contrasted strongly with Mel's gentle laughter.

Mel managed to get a hold of herself. "I'm sorry, Mephi, but Luce probably has a good case against Persi for sexual harassment. As I understand it, all the unwanted invitations were made by her, and she persevered, despite numerous refusals."

Mephi's expression was one of disbelief. Her eyes rested on Luce.

"All right, once," Luce snapped. "She'd been begging to give me a blowjob for a week. She was on her knees and she already had me out of my pants. I figured if I let her, maybe she'd shut up for a few minutes." He sneaked a glance at Mel, praying she wouldn't reject him for his momentary weakness.

To his shock, Mel burst out laughing. "If there's one thing I taught Persi, it's not to talk with her mouth full."

Luce felt himself reddening under the combined weight of Mel's amused and Mephi's disapproving gazes. Did Mel think so little of him that she found it no surprise that he would sleep around at the slightest invitation? Or had Persephone already told her? What else had the nephilim said? Had she belittled his size and skill and stamina? She'd told plenty of other lies about him – why not that? His hands itched to wrap around the girl's neck and choke the life from her.

"But first we have to find her and that's why we're here," Mel continued. "Mephi, please give us a summary of what you know, so we can plan how to proceed."

Mephi nodded and flipped open the file with a shapely talon. "Three weeks ago, she was scheduled to fly to Heathrow. I booked the flights myself and I saw her in the office only a few hours before her departure. It's the last time I saw Miss Black. Her frequent-flyer miles indicate that she boarded the flight, but I have no record of London accommodation. Her credit card statement for the following day shows a purchase in something called Asda Omagh."

"Where?" Mel's suddenly alert pose mirrored Mephi's. "Asda where?"

"Omagh. It's in Northern Ireland. And I have a note from her telling me she was expecting a call from someone named Patrick. I never received it, so he must have called her back direct. That's the last day of her credit card statement and the next one's not due for another fortnight, so I don't know any more about her transactions. She hasn't sent a single email since she left the country."

Mel rose. "I need to call Patrick. Mephi, can

you please book flights for next week? Looks like Luce and I are headed to London. Oh, and please find out if Bob can be the acting CEO during our absence. Luce, can you get me a list of your business contacts in the UK and Ireland? If Persi's there for business, I'm sure she'll have spoken to at least one of them. Who would she know?"

London? But weren't he and Mel needed here with the HELL Corporation? Luce tried to wrap his head around her sprinting thought processes and fell even further behind. "She'd know the government officials we met in London. That's all."

Mel nodded. "Fine. I'll arrange our accommodation in London."

Mephi coughed. "I usually take care of that. I have a list of Mr Iblis' preferred London hotels. I'll arrange a suite for each of you so you have all the privacy you need." She eyed Luce, as if expecting him to argue.

"That won't be necessary, Mephi," Mel said. "I prefer to stay in my friend's flat in Knightsbridge, where there'll be plenty of room for Luce and myself. Let me know what dates you can book flights for. Luce, please tell me when your contacts can meet with us. We'll need to arrive the day before the meeting, I think."

"Do I have to go?" Luce asked. He wanted to avoid the nephilim as much as possible.

"Yes," Mel responded. "Your business contacts there will expect to meet with you and not some girl they've never met before. It's not all bad. You'll have one of your wishes granted." He perked up but she continued before he could say a word, "I'll be your PA for the day."

Luce jumped and whooped, to Mephi's shocked disapproval. "And how personal will your assistance get?"

He raised suggestive eyebrows.

"Mr Iblis!" Mephi exploded.

Eighteen

"The spare key is…here," murmured Mel, feeling around the doorframe. The key was dusty but functional, as she demonstrated by turning it in the lock. The door opened silently – a tiny crack revealing more light inside than the dim passage where they stood. "If you take our bags in, I'll put the key back and be right behind you."

Luce shouldered the door open and wheeled both suitcases into the tiny entrance hall. The bags thumped behind him as he dragged them up the stairs.

On her tiptoes, trying to stick the key back behind the moulding, Mel heard Luce's voice call, "Ah, Mel? Is this supposed to be here?"

"Is what supposed to be here?" she asked, trudging up the stairs after him. Her exhausted steps were slower than normal – she needed a good sleep after such a long flight. "The one thing I want most is a bed and as long as there's one of those, I'm in Heaven already."

Luce made space for her on the landing where he stood, staring. "A near-naked man wearing a skirt and drinking Scotch on the sofa."

Mel's face lit up. "Patrick!" She stumbled across the carpet to give the shirtless Patrick a hug. And a kiss, to Luce's smouldering anger.

"I couldn't sit on the other side of the Irish Sea and not come to see you, knowing you were so close. I wanted to congratulate you personally – and hear the story from your own lovely lips. Of course, I dressed for the occasion." He gestured at his tartan kilt. "I even brought a bottle of my best to loosen those lips a little." He waved at the whisky on the table and the empty glass beside it.

Luce squinted at the label. "There's a Laphroaig I haven't tasted." He crossed to the table and poured a little into the glass, lifting it to his nose. "It sure smells good." He savoured a small sip before saying, "Now that's something I'd happily wait a quarter of a century for." He held out the glass to Mel. "You should taste this. I want to take a bottle home with me."

Patrick laughed heartily. "Well, at least the devil has good taste. And he knows how to treat a lady. Maybe this is one snake I'll tolerate – even share a house with, though I wish you'd warned me, *Mel meum*." He waved at the well-muscled torso Mel admired. "I might've put on a shirt."

Mel's laughter was gentler by far. "I wasn't sure how you'd react, Patrick. Some people are so hostile to Luce that it's easier not to mention him in advance. Even Raphael's been rather rude – I had to reprimand him over it. It's not like any of us are perfect and it seems that Luce has a talent for revealing all our imperfections in the most unpleasant ways."

She stepped forward to take the glass Luce offered, before inhaling and drinking deeply.

Both men watched her blissful face as she held the liquid in her mouth before swallowing. Mel's eyes darted from Patrick's slightly lifted kilt to Luce shifting uncomfortably in his pants as if he wanted to loosen them. She sighed deeply. "I'm really looking forward to drinking more of this with both of you boys. Luce tells a tale at least as well as I do and most likely better, but it's been a very long flight, so I'd really like the storytelling session to wait until after I've had a lot more sleep. Please, Patrick — which guest room is ours?"

Patrick seemed to hesitate for only a moment before saying, "Your room is the same as always, *Mel meum*. I can prepare another room for Lucifer, if you like. All I'll need to do is get some fresh linen." His eyes stayed on Mel, as if he knew that Luce himself would have no say in the matter.

Mel set her empty glass down. "One room is plenty, thank you." She turned to Luce. "Can you bring the suitcases, my love? I know you probably don't need to sleep, but I'd like it if you could stay with me until I drift off."

"If that's what you want," Luce replied, following her down the hall until they reached the bedroom. He closed the bedroom door behind him, only to discover that Mel hadn't waited for privacy before pulling her clothes off. Luce stood with his back to the door, admiring the view. When she was down to her knickers, he couldn't resist any more – he crossed the room in two strides to wrap his arms around her, pulling her in close for a kiss.

Mel responded, but she was slow and uncharacteristically clumsy. "I'm sorry, Luce. I'm so tired that I can barely stand any more. I should…find my pjs and sleep…" she yawned, "but I want a cup of…"

"I'll get it," Luce interrupted. "Let me help you to bed first." For the second, precious time, he lifted her into bed. She seemed almost as tired as she'd been the first time – after she'd walked naked through Hell for him and fallen asleep on his bathroom floor. One more kiss and he left in search of the kitchen.

Nineteen

Patrick was in the kitchen already and still only wearing his tartan skirt.

"Do you have any…?" Luce stopped as Patrick pointed to a mug of milk on the bench. It hadn't been there long – it still had bubbles on top from the turbulence of being poured from the bottle. "Thanks." He returned to Mel, mug in hand.

Mel was almost asleep already, but sat up to gulp down the contents of the cup before handing it back to Luce. "Thank you." She sank back into the pillow, reaching for him. "Lie with me for a few minutes?"

Luce kicked off his shoes and stretched out behind her, spooning nice and close. Mel gave a contented sigh and settled against him. "I love you," he said softly.

"Mmm, love you, too," she mumbled.

Luce didn't have long to wait before Mel's breathing slowed to her normal sleeping rhythm. Carefully, he levered himself off the bed and returned to the kitchen.

Patrick was still there, sipping his whisky. "Want one?" he asked, pulling a clean glass from the overhead cupboard. Luce nodded. Patrick poured two fingers' worth for him and picked up his own drink again. "To Mel getting a good night's sleep," he said, waiting for Luce to raise his glass before drinking.

Luce took his time savouring the taste before he swallowed. "If you've poisoned it, I think I'll still drink the rest. This is too good to waste."

"I'd not poison something as good as this. The alcohol in it is poison enough for me. If I wanted to add something to it, I'd give you the cheap stuff and not my best. Besides, you're hers. I'd never do something against her wishes."

"How'd you know about the milk?" Luce asked.

Patrick grinned. "She's a lady with particular tastes and they don't change. At least I didn't have to go out into the ice and snow to milk a goat for it this time. I bet she didn't sleep on the plane at all, either."

"She insisted on economy class and spent the whole time just listening to the other passengers, she said, as she planned what to do when we landed. I could've paid for first class tickets so she could sleep, but she wouldn't hear of it." Luce shook his head. "What are you to her?"

"I'm me. I manage the UK and Ireland, helping out with Europe as necessary. I do…whatever Mel asks me to do. And I always will." Another grin, another sip and the saint didn't continue.

Luce felt his frustration build. Getting information out of this angel was like trying to seduce Mel when he'd still been a demon.

"Have you slept with her?" he blurted out, betting he wouldn't get a straight answer.

"Whenever she asks me to – of course. Same as you," Patrick said. He laughed. "You think I'd be wandering around wearing nothing but my kilt if it weren't for her? I never wore one of these things when I was alive. I wore one to an official meeting once, where I met her. Oh, centuries ago now. I've been hers ever since. I've only met one of her other close friends – a Japanese fellow named Koyane. She meets up with him whenever she's in Japan, Korea and occasionally China. No idea how many she has – not enough, I'm sure, though I can name plenty who'd be willing. She's very particular about who she chooses."

"An angel with a harem of fuck buddies? I never picked Mel for someone who'd keep a man in every port."

Patrick's eyes turned shrewd. "Is that what you think you are to her? She'd never put it so crudely, but I suspect she relies on you more than you realise. She wouldn't have brought you here with her without some reason for it. She wouldn't trust you if she didn't know you were hers – mind, body and soul."

"What, like some sort of minion? Is she building an army to take over Heaven or something? Because it'll never work. I've tried that and…I swore I'd never do it again. She wouldn't be stupid enough to…"

Patrick laughed. "Do you even know who she is?"

"She's Mel. Lady Muriel of the Hashmallim. The one woman – the only angel – I'd do anything for," Luce replied, annoyed. "Of course I know who she is."

"Lady Muriel, leader of the Hashmallim. The angel in charge of keeping order in all the realms of this world. Earth, Heaven and Hell. I heard she took charge of your little patch only recently, so perhaps you didn't know the rest, for she's left you to yourself for longer than I thought she would. She doesn't need an army to take control of Heaven. She manages it already. Oh, there are angels that outrank her in other respects, but she's the one who runs the place." He eyed Luce. "It's setting an army against Heaven without her at your side that's stupid."

Luce felt the desire building to punch the angel, breaking his perfect nose or blackening one of those green eyes. But that meant he'd have to heal the man afterwards, or explain to Mel in the morning. Being a demon was much easier than being an angel again, he fumed.

Patrick seemed to sense his thoughts. "I'm sorry if that came across as insensitive. I wasn't born when you had your battle for Heaven. I don't share the bitterness that other angels have. I only know what I've heard – and that Mel wasn't there. She doesn't open up to many, you know. She's sweet and kind to everyone, but she doesn't share herself much. Her thoughts, her feelings, her doubts…her vulnerabilities. If she trusts you, I must, too. It doesn't matter who you are, what you've done or if we've fought as bitter enemies in the past. No one reads souls as clearly as she does. If she thinks you're worthy of her trust…then you have mine." He raised his glass and tipped the last of the contents into his mouth.

Luce lifted his in response. "This is way too civilised. Shouldn't we be fighting it out for her, like a couple of testosterone-fuelled humans? Aren't you even the slightest bit jealous that she wants to sleep with me instead of you?" He thought the angel looked uneasy for the first time, but it was barely perceptible.

Patrick shrugged, his smile never leaving his face. "She chooses who she wants and I will always be available if she needs me. Mel knows that. What she needs most now is someone to take care of her – someone who'll offer what she needs because she'll never ask. She looked so stressed the last time I saw her in Sri Lanka. She was worrying about you when she should have been resting. I tried to get her to relax a little, but even the days I had with her weren't enough for her to recharge properly. Maybe I shouldn't have taken her fishing…but how was I to know she'd catch a monster fighting fish?"

Sri Lanka. Fishing. Luce's thoughts darted to the photos of the one holiday Mel had taken from the HELL Corporation. "You went to Sri Lanka with her?" Jealousy bit at his insides.

"No, I met her there after the conference, for less than two days before our flights were scheduled to leave. Did she show you the photos I took?" Patrick asked. "She still seemed sad when she left. She's happier now, but…more tired, too. Maybe it's just the long flight and she'll look healthier once she's had a good night's sleep or three. If she doesn't, you need to take better care of her or I'll step in. Your ego takes second place to Mel. She's too important."

Luce swore he'd take Mel on a proper holiday when they got back. No fishing. Just…whatever she wanted.

"She's everything to me. Everyone else just seems to want to make life harder for the two of us. You might be the first person who wants to help her instead of trying to pry us apart. I think I'm beginning to like you, angel. If she trusts you…" He drank. "And you have damn good taste in whisky. I wondered where Mel developed her taste for the stuff. She didn't have a drop of alcohol in her house when I turned up…tried to warm me up with tea!"

"I bet it worked, too. Something from a teapot without any milk that tasted surprisingly good. She knows exactly what to do…and she hardly needs alcohol to help someone relax! I'll never be as good as she is, but she's had millennia of practice." Patrick winked. "Was she fast asleep when you left her?"

Luce nodded. "Out like a light. She'll probably sleep for at least the next eight hours, if not more. Don't tell her, but I'm definitely going to try to get us first class seats for the flight home. It was heartbreaking, seeing the state she was in when we landed after going so long without sleep. I thought I was going to have to carry her as well as the suitcases. If I surprise her, maybe she'll agree to take the seats instead of finding a way to torture herself again."

"If she's as deeply asleep as you say, then she already knows. No need for me to tell her. You should, though – tell her you want to give her luxury to take care of her. She'll understand that and she might even agree. Right, Mel?" He paused, as if waiting for her to reply, but she didn't appear or make a sound. "She's the best soul-reader, but she's also a skilled spirit-walker. Once her body was resting properly, she'd have come right back here to listen to us and make sure we weren't ripping shreds off each other. I doubt she missed much." Patrick grinned. "So, tell me, Lucifer, former demon and Lord of Hell. Can you see her?"

Luce stared at the man, then searched the room, looking for signs that they weren't alone. He closed his eyes, seeking with his other senses, too – but found nothing and no one else. Tossing up between telling the truth and saying nothing at all, he wished he could lie like a demon again. "No," he admitted finally. "Can you?"

Patrick hesitated. "No, I can't. And I won't unless she wants me to. I thought…the rumours said she'd bonded with you, so maybe you'd be able to. I guess the rumours were wrong."

Luce didn't know what to say. After so long not trusting anyone, it was hard to place his trust in this stranger, no matter how much Mel took him into her confidence. "I think Mel wanted us to wait before telling tales of Hell. She wanted to be awake." He downed the last of his whisky, relishing the burn as it descended. "I know it's early, but I think I might need rest almost as much as she does. It was a long flight." He gave Patrick a nod and headed back to the room he shared with Mel.

She hadn't moved, so he stripped and slid into bed beside her. Sleep ambushed him soon after.

Twenty

Mel's silky skin slid over Luce's as her warm weight settled on top of him. She laid a line of kisses across his chest before angling upward to claim his lips. Her tongue tickled his, inviting him to give her everything. And he wanted to. God, how much he wanted to.

Dreams didn't come any better than this.

Gentle laughter accompanied the softness of her lips on his neck. "You're not dreaming, my love."

Luce pried his eyes open. Sunlight from the

casement windows haloed his precious angel, who was perched on top of him with every glorious curve on display.

"The most Heavenly wake-up call ever," he mumbled.

She wet her lips. "I think I might be able to improve on it."

Oh God she was good…

"Good morning. Looks like you brought a tiny bit of sunlight with you. I bet that won't last – London weather's horrible on a good day."

Luce squinted at the doorway, which framed a cheerful Patrick. Didn't the saint care that he was interrupting an intimate moment?

"I'd hoped to be at your disposal today, but somehow SIS heard about my arrival and I've been dragged over to Downing Street for meetings all day," Patrick continued, seemingly oblivious. "I insisted I couldn't stay past five, though, so I'll be home for dinner and I'd like to make it up to you by taking you to a place nearby that does the most exquisite venison. If David needs me past five, then he'll just have to join us. Good luck today!" The door clicked shut behind him.

The blankets screening Mel's nakedness slipped off her shoulders as Luce let go. "Hasn't he ever heard of knocking?" Luce grumbled.

Mel laughed softly. "Probably, but I think he's so excited I'm here that he forgot. Never mind. We still have plenty of time before we need to get up. The meeting's not until ten, right?"

Grudgingly, Luce confirmed it. And with the flat to themselves, maybe he could persuade Mel to make a little noise…

When they did stumble out of bed some time later, Mel headed straight for the shower while Luce searched the kitchen for coffee. He was still staring suspiciously at the jar of instant coffee, wondering if he could stand to choke it down, when Mel emerged.

She buttoned the pale grey jacket over her smoke-coloured shirt, so that the suit accentuated her curves perfectly while presenting clean lines that said she was all business. "Patrick knows I have a taste for the croissants from the patisserie downstairs, so he'll probably have left some in the fridge." She tugged the fridge door open and set the bakery box on the bench. "More than enough for both of us."

Luce barely tasted his breakfast. He couldn't keep his eyes off Mel – he'd never seen her wear these clothes before. Even the aqua scarf she tied at her throat was new to him. When she leaned over to put on her shoes, he couldn't resist her any more.

Mel carefully peeled his hand off her arse. "Luce, this is a business meeting. We have to remain professional for at least a few hours. When it's over, then you can misbehave."

"I can't help it," he replied, devouring her with his eyes instead. "Your skirt is taunting me. It's moulded so perfectly to your body that it's making me jealous."

She laughed. "Luce, you're staring at my bum again."

He wanted to apologise, but he knew he'd be lying if he said he was sorry. "We should probably get going," he said instead.

When they arrived, a secretary ushered them straight through to a meeting room where three men already waited.

"Andy, Charles, Alexander," Luce said as he shook hands with each of them. 'This is Mel." He waved her forward and reined in his jealousy as each man took her hand.

"What happened to your old PA? The cheeky brunette?" Andy asked as he ensconced himself on a chair.

Luce's heart sank. They wouldn't be asking after Persephone if they'd met with her recently. "I expected her to travel here and meet with you. I take it she hasn't?"

Three heads shook.

"We'll just have to manage without her. It seems she's not as useful as I'd hoped." Luce gave a bland smile. "That's why Mel's here."

Charles grinned, dragging his chair closer to the table. "But the last one had such a firm grasp of the principles behind a national system like ours."

Luce tried not to stare. Is that how Persephone had managed to negotiate such favourable terms in the UK? Had she seduced the government officials, too?

Mel cleared her throat. "I believe in this

case, we require more than just a firm grasp on what lies behind. In order for this relationship to work, the HELL Corporation must have an intimate knowledge of the anatomy of the entire system, both inside and out. That, Director General, is why I'm here." The serene smile never left her face.

Luce melted. That voice and that tone and…

Mel's hand clamped over his before his fingers could creep any higher up her thigh. The others didn't look like they'd noticed a thing – they seemed to be sharing similar thoughts to the fantasy spinning through Luce's head, though they couldn't know Mel's body anywhere near as well as he did.

Alexander recovered first. "That sounds ambitious, so perhaps we'd best get started."

Within fifteen minutes, Luce had started to doze. Mel's gentle nudge under the table brought him back to the present, but it didn't seem to be more interesting than the contents of his own head. With Mel's help, he managed to keep his eyes open for the rest of the meeting, but it was a challenge. Negotiating the agreements between the UK government and the HELL Corporation was one thing, but hashing out all the details was so tedious he swore he'd make underlings deal with it for every other contract he'd secured or he'd murder someone. Was there any chance Mel would be willing to…

Mel gave a tiny head-shake.

After what seemed like forever – which, according to Luce's watch was really less than two hours – Mel said, "Thank you, gentlemen. I think that pretty much covers the groundwork for our relationship. I'll take my notes back to the office and get some of our staff to work on the details. Once we're done, I'll see to it that you're sent the complete proposal." She gathered her papers and tucked them into her folder. Her fingers stroked the golden-brown leather once and were still.

"I like your new PA, Iblis," Charles said as he reached across the table to shake Luce's hand. His eyes darted pointedly to Luce's other hand, still sitting on Mel's thigh. "Is she as accommodating as the last one?"

Mel's eyes dropped demurely to the desk as

if she was flattered. She couldn't have caught the innuendo, then, Luce decided. But he sure had.

Luce's anger flamed into life. Mel wasn't accommodating – any attention she gave him was Heaven-sent, not some sordid workplace flirtation. "Mel isn't my PA. She's agreed to be the Chief Financial Officer at the HELL Corporation as a personal favour to me."

Mel rose. "I apologise. I thought you gentlemen remembered me, so no introduction would be necessary. It was my mistake. I'm Murielle D'Angelo. As Luce said, temporary CFO in HELL."

Alexander's eyes narrowed as if he recognised her name, but couldn't seem to work out why. The other two men didn't seem to know her at all.

"I fulfil a similar role in Asia, the Middle East and the Pacific to what Patrick Driscoll does in the UK and Eire," Mel added.

Andy's eyes lit up. "Driscoll's your mentor?"

Luce laughed. "I think you'll find it's the other way around. When Patrick needs help, he calls Mel. Just like I did." He watched as

Mel's hand was clasped between each man's for much longer this time, while each looked her squarely in the eye as they thanked her for her time.

Twenty-one

Mel tucked her arm through Luce's as they walked onto Whitehall. When he tried to turn left, she tugged him to the right. "I don't want to take the Tube. It's only a couple of miles. I want to walk. All the gardens and old buildings on the way…it's been a long time since I've been in London and it's so green." She paused, then added, "Plus, we'll probably find somewhere nicer to buy lunch than on the underground."

He agreed and soon they were headed along

an avenue of pale-trunked trees, the branches overhead only just starting to show their feathery spring leaves.

Mel sighed contentedly, breathing out her tension with every step. She hadn't been prepared to run today's meeting, expecting Luce to do that instead of daydreaming. A lot had happened since she'd talked Persi through the initial negotiations that had secured the contract in the first place, and she hadn't been so tired then. She'd let Luce and even Patrick believe that her exhaustion was because of the flight, but she knew better. Mel was soul-weary to the point of needing a sabbatical, and soon.

If only there wasn't so much to do. Persi was still missing. The HELL Corporation needed better senior management. Luce required a mentor to help him learn to be an angel again after so long. And then there was…

Mel's thoughts were dragged back to the present as Luce pinned her to a tree. "What are you doing?" she asked, giving him a gentle push.

"The skies just opened up and you're

soaked," he replied.

Mel lifted her sleeve and stared in wonder. He was right, she realised, watching rainwater trickle down her fingers to the pavement. She shivered. Being soaked in spring in Australia was one thing; here in London it was a much more serious matter. How could she have forgotten where she was? She hadn't even brought an umbrella. Mel closed her eyes. She was so tired she was slipping. Even her thoughts were sluggish as she racked her brain, trying to remember what she should do.

Finally, she said, "Can you get a cab for us?" Her eyes fixed on his, praying that she was right in trusting Luce to take care of her. Was it too soon? He'd been an angel again for such a short time and demons weren't known for their helpfulness. Especially when an angel showed signs of weakness.

"Of course." The comforting heat of his body vanished as he approached the kerb, pulling her along with him. He hailed a cab and helped her inside, then sat beside her and hugged her close for the short drive back to Patrick's place. She jerked awake from her light doze when the car stopped, shocked that she'd slept. Why was she so weary? What had she done? Was this the result of the energy burst that had destroyed those dark souls? She'd certainly stay away from Hell for a bit, then, until she felt better.

Mel stumbled up the stairs after Luce, debating whether she was more tired today than she'd been upon their arrival yesterday. A flight without sleep was nothing compared to today's meeting, slipping in and out of three men's thoughts as she strove to ensure the meeting ran smoothly. And all the while wondering where Persi was.

"Let's get you out of those wet clothes," Luce murmured, unbuttoning her jacket and peeling it from her soaked shirt.

Uncontrollable shivering made her teeth chatter, making it an effort for her to get the words out. "Always tr-trying to get me naked. You got drenched, too, Luce. Why aren't you shivering?"

He grinned and shucked off his jacket and shirt. Carefully licking his finger, he ran it down his chiselled chest. A wisp of steam curled up and Luce chuckled. "Because I'm your hot, sexy devil, that's why. Of course I want you naked. A hot shower will help, but it's pretty pointless with clothes on."

Mel nodded and stepped into the warm spray, lifting her closed eyes to Heaven as Luce crowded in behind her. Hard muscles pressed against her back as his arms circled her waist.

"Sorry about the hard-on, Mel, but you know what your body does to me," he whispered in her ear. "I swear I'll wait until you're warm before I even consider suggesting sex."

"That'll be hard for you," Mel blurted out before she'd really considered the words.

Luce kissed the top of her head, laughing softly. "Yes it will, but taking care of you comes first. Before my ego and my libido."

Patrick's words from last night, Mel thought muzzily. So Luce had been listening to him after all.

The warm body supporting hers let go and Mel leaned against the tiles as she regained her balance.

"I'll go find you some dry clothes. You stay

under the hot water, okay?"

"Mm."

Luce seemed to take this as agreement or at least acknowledgement and he left.

The water flow ceased, forcing Mel to open her eyes. A warm towel brushed against her back, then draped across her shoulders. Automatically, she pulled the edges around herself to leach some of the warmth into her body.

Firm hands rubbed the soft flannel against her skin, wicking away the water. "Mel, are you all right?" Luce asked.

She looked up into his concerned eyes. Now or never, she decided. Time to find out what a reformed demon did with a weakened angel. "No. I'm too tired." If this was a mistake, at least Patrick would be home in a few hours to take care of her.

"So you'd like me to help you to bed?"

Her head wasn't working right. Too lethargic to think. "I don't know."

Luce looked lost for a moment, but he recovered quickly. "How about I help you get dressed and you can rest on the couch while I arrange some lunch for us?"

Mel nodded.

Her clumsy fingers hindered more than helped as Luce dressed her in some of her comfortable winter clothes that lived here in London most of the time, but he didn't make a single complaint. Instead, he swept her up in his arms and carried her to the modular sofa in the lounge room.

Luce dropped to his knees beside her so their eyes were level. "Will you be okay here for bit while I head out to get you something for lunch? I might be able to rustle up something in the kitchen, but the chances of it being edible are pretty slim. Unless you want an omelette."

Mel summoned a smile. "There are no eggs. I checked this morning. I'll be fine. I'll just…sleep a little, maybe."

Luce nodded. "This isn't just because of the flight yesterday, is it?"

For the first time, she cursed the angelic requirement to tell the truth. Luce didn't need the additional burden of knowing how much his rescue from Hell had taxed her. "No."

His lips brushed lightly against hers. "You rest until I come back. I want to know what can turn my invincible angel into a shadow of herself."

Mel nodded and sank into the couch cushions. Sleep was just a whisper away.

Twenty-two

Why was it so cold? Mel reached for the blankets to pull them over her head, but found none. Blinking, she looked around. The darkening sky outside the window told her it was evening, but she couldn't remember having lunch. She'd somehow fallen asleep on the sofa but she was colder now than she'd been that morning.

"I thought you were going to sleep all afternoon," Luce said, his touch tingling as he stroked her hair.

Tingling…healing…he'd been healing her as she lay unconscious. Well, that sure answered her question about whether he'd help her or cause more trouble while she was weak, but it didn't explain the chilly inside air. On the other hand, she certainly felt more like herself. Luce's healing ability was improving.

"You should have woken me," she said, sitting up. "What happened to lunch?"

"In the fridge. I figured I'd heat yours up when you woke."

Mel nodded and rose stiffly to her feet. "Why's it so cold in here?"

Luce shrugged. "It is? I didn't notice."

Shaking her head, Mel hurried to the bedroom and shrugged into her winter coat. Luce wasn't in the lounge room when she returned, so she followed the sound of swearing to the kitchen. "What is it?"

Luce held out his finger. "Paper cut from the tea box."

Mel laughed and healed him with a touch. "Tea would help."

"I figured whisky would warm you up pretty well, too, but I wasn't sure which you'd prefer." Luce nudged the glass on the bench and the aroma of aged whisky wafted Mel's way.

She breathed deeply. "That's Patrick's new one, the bottle you boys were drinking last night, isn't it? So you two didn't finish it off while I was asleep." She lifted the glass and sniffed. "Now I know why you boys didn't argue. Wouldn't want to spill a drop of this." She sipped it and sighed with pleasure. "I should have tea, but I haven't had whisky this good in a while." Carefully, she drank half of it, then handed the glass to Luce. "You should have some, too, so I'm not drinking alone. Thank you for taking such good care of me."

He looked gratified. "Of course I took care of you. With all you do for me, how could I not return the favour? It wasn't exactly a hardship. I got to undress you, share your shower, and hold you in my arms. Any time, Melody, I'd do anything for you." He drank some of her whisky. "Damn, that's good. See? I even get to share great whisky with you. Now, I should probably heat up your lunch. Are you hungry?"

Mel glanced at her watch. "Yes, but Patrick said he'd be done by five and it's close to that now. He'll be back within the hour and then we'll go out for dinner. I'll be fine to wait, as long as he isn't late."

A door slammed downstairs, followed by the thunder of running footsteps on old wooden stairs. "You're talking about me, aren't you?" Patrick called up. "Well, that's funny, because you're the one on everyone's lips today. The Chief of MI6 or whatever they're called now almost dragged me out of the Prime Minister's office to interrogate me about you. Wanted to know how I knew Ms D'Angelo…or as he called her, the Angel of Afghanistan." He reached for a glass and poured himself some whisky. "Care to explain?"

Mel permitted herself a small smile. "He was the senior British intelligence officer stationed in Afghanistan. I'm surprised he didn't recognise me this morning. He must have a lot on his plate at the moment. It was nothing unusual. You know me in war, Patrick. I…help."

"Help?" Luce repeated darkly.

Mel laid a hand on his arm. "It's what I do best. I help wars end and I try to minimise the casualties during the conflict. Afghanistan was actually easier than Iraq, which isn't saying much. It was the sand that got to me most. Now, I managed to skip lunch, so is there any chance you boys will agree to have an early dinner on my account? Patrick, you mentioned venison and I've been trying to work out how long it's been since I tasted it. You know what? I don't know. I must have forgotten."

Patrick grinned. "Let me get out of my work clothes and we can go. You might want to change, too, Mel – this one's a fancy restaurant and you know how Londoners get."

Mel glanced down. Yes, she did know how Londoners got. Sighing, she headed for the bedroom to find a suitable dress for dinner.

Patrick called after her, "Don't take too long primping. I'm starving, and after dinner I'm dying to hear all about your adventures in Hell."

Twenty-three

Patrick reached for the bottle of wine. "I still can't believe you brought ping pong balls into Hell, Mel. I'm going to be laughing about that one for ages. Every time I think about it." Red wine glugged into his glass. He held the bottle out to Luce. "More?"

Luce glanced at his nearly full glass and shook his head. He'd lost track of how much he'd had to drink, but it wasn't like he'd be driving. All he had to do was stumble down the passage to bed. He could crawl and still make it.

"She's the only angel to ever make it all the way through Hell unscathed, and out again, too," Luce said, raising his glass before he gulped half of it down. "Nothing short of miraculous, that's Melody."

"An angel in Hell." Patrick burst out laughing, still shaking his head. "No one else would have dared…and you just walked in there. Mel, what were you thinking?"

Mel was strangely silent.

"Mel?"

Both Patrick and Luce stared at her. Mel's eyes were closed and her even breathing was the only sound in the silent flat.

"She's fallen asleep," Patrick breathed. "Must take something pretty important for her to just leave without a word like that. Best get her body to bed and be ready to help if she needs us. I hope it's not another bomb in the Tube…"

Something didn't seem right. "No. She's here." Luce leaned over. "Melody, wake up, sweetheart." He kissed her and felt her respond, so he kissed her again.

"You're a braver man than I am," Patrick remarked.

Luce ignored him, keeping every bit of his focus on Mel. Her lips were moving under his and her eyelids fluttered. Reluctantly, he pulled away, but his eyes didn't leave her face.

Mel sighed and smiled. "That was…the sweetest way to wake up. Thank you. I…I didn't mean to doze off like that. I was listening to you telling Patrick about the strange supernova you saw and didn't realise my body had slipped into unconsciousness."

Luce stroked her hair. "It's okay. It's probably not half as exciting to you. You didn't see a girl turn into a star."

Patrick cleared his throat. "Mel, you passed out. I figured you were off saving half of London, but he knew different. Care to explain? Is it true – you and him…" His voice seemed to die on him.

Twenty-four

"Bonded," Mel said softly. "Our souls are bonded. The night Luce became an angel again. I'd never have found him in Hell if we weren't."

"Why?" Patrick croaked out. "He'd barely been an angel for five minutes, Mel!"

Luce had wondered exactly the same thing, but he'd never dared to ask her. Now was his chance to find out.

Luce felt Mel's fingers grasp his hand and squeeze. Her body stiffened as she kept her eyes on Patrick. "Because I love him. Because he'd invited me deep into his soul and I didn't want to break such a powerful connection with a kindred spirit. Because I was selfish and I didn't want to let go of the soul I loved." She blew out a breath. "Not after I'd had to give him up once for Persi." A warm drop of liquid landed on Luce's arm, followed by several more. She was crying, he realised.

He wrapped his arms around her, the precious angel who loved him. "Since when? When did you know?" The words were out before Luce realised he'd opened his mouth.

Mel sniffled. "I don't know. I believe it started at the office picnic, but I didn't realise until after you left with Persi. I…I travelled to New York one night to check on you both, and it broke my heart to leave you in that state. Persi called me every day after that and I told her how to take care of you. From your coffee to your meals to your shirts and your schedule and everything I could think of. She wanted so much to be an angel that she begged to take my place in HELL so she could prove herself. And Raphael agreed, so I stepped back."

Luce snorted at his own stupidity in not seeing it before. "It was you. The whole time, it was you. The first week with Persephone was maddening, she was so useless. And then it was like she learned and improved…but she didn't really, did she? Everything she did was on your advice." Triumph kindled in his chest. Mel had wanted him – she hadn't been immune to his charms after all. The constant offers of sex from the nephilim had come from Mel!

Mel laughed weakly. "Not everything."

Luce waited with bated breath.

"She's the one who wanted to go to bed with you. I had no advice for her on that subject, though she asked enough times."

Luce's heart plummeted. Had none of his amorous advances in the office affected Mel at all? Wait, there'd been the time Persi had…

"And I've never given a man oral sex in my life. That's definitely Persi's speciality, or so I've heard."

Shit. Even Luce's fantasies, wishing the lamprey who'd blown him had been Mel, crumbled into dust.

Patrick burst out laughing. "I'm not sure what's funnier. Hearing you talk about blowjobs or seeing his hopes for one wither and die in his expression." Under Mel's gaze, the saint sobered and stood. "I'll go get some more drinks, shall I?" He gathered the glasses and retreated to the kitchen.

Mel's soft voice was barely audible. "I'm sorry, Luce. If I'd known how much trouble Persi would cause with my assistance, I'd never have let her accompany you. And I shouldn't…shouldn't have sealed the bond without asking you first. If you want to dissolve the bond between us, tell me and I'll do it. I'll help find you another mentor to replace me so that you don't have to even look at me again if you don't want to. I did what I did because I wanted your soul and because I love you. You have no obligation to me and I thank you for everything –"

"Hold up," Luce interrupted. "What are you talking about? Breaking bonds and foisting me on someone else?" His heart froze. "Am I too much trouble for you, Mel? Please, I know I'm rusty at being an angel, but I'll try harder, I swear. Please don't dissolve anything. Please, Mel. As I recall, I begged you on my knees for your help that night and I'll do it again. Nothing has made me happier than this bond, or whatever it is we share. You raised me from the depths of Hell because of it. I owe you more than anything for what you've done for me. And I will repay you, in any way I can." He kissed her, praying desperately that she wouldn't pull away. She'd risked everything for him in Heaven, Hell and on Earth and all the realms were empty without her. "I love you, Melody, and NOTHING will change that."

She smiled through her tears and Luce's heart dared to beat again.

"Even if you don't know how to give a blowjob," he continued.

Mel let out a very un-angelic snort.

"With a bit of instruction and a lot of practice, maybe you could –"

"Luce!" Whatever else she'd meant to say was lost in her helpless laughter.

Twenty-five

"Mel?" Patrick said quietly. He approached her, cupping a mug between his hands.

Luce wondered what had happened to the drinks Patrick had volunteered to get for them. It looked like he'd decided to cater for just himself.

To his surprise, Patrick held the mug out to Mel. She took the frothy milk without saying a word, but she didn't lift it to her lips.

"Please permit me to read your soul," Patrick continued, his hands hovering over

Mel's. She nodded once and his hands wrapped around hers even as she held the mug.

Jealousy raged in Luce's guts like a demon trying to wrestle its way out. Mel had given her permission, but he didn't like the saint touching her one little bit.

Patrick released her. "Mel, you should be in Heaven, not here." He looked straight at Luce. "You should take her there. Help her conserve the precious little she has left."

"No," Mel murmured. "I have too much to do to waste time in Heaven right now. When this situation is resolved…"

"Let me. Let Raphael. Let someone else handle it. If you keep going like this, you'll be forced to do it anyway and you won't be able to choose when you go."

Luce felt his irritation build at the angel's perpetual riddles. "Let you what? No one's forcing Mel to do anything and I'd love to see someone try. I will do whatever she says I need to do, and if Mel says she doesn't want to go to Heaven, I'm not taking her anywhere."

"Does he know?" Patrick pressed. Mel made

no movement or reply. He turned his eyes on Luce. "Do you know how exhausted she is? Even her soul is drained of energy, almost to the point of not being able to maintain that body. She desperately needs rest."

Mel drank deeply and Luce felt her body move with each swallow.

"I know she's tired," Luce replied. "More tired than I've ever seen her. I thought it was just the flight, but –"

The mug smacked down on the coffee table. "I'm fine. Tired, yes, but not so decrepit that I'm going to disintegrate before your eyes if I so much as take a deeper breath than usual. Luce is taking care of me. Today was…very draining…but I'll rest until we leave London. I have time to recuperate before our flight home. I'm sure I'll…you don't need to do that!" Startled, Luce eased up on healing her. He'd only been trying to restore her body – he didn't know where to start with healing a soul. He would if he could, though. "But thank you," she finished softly.

"Do you want me to take you to bed?" Luce asked.

Mel shifted and winced. "Probably for the best," she admitted.

Luce didn't wait for her to say more. He lifted her easily in his arms and carried her to their room. He shoved aside the covers to lay her on the bed before pulling the quilt up over her. "Is there anything else I can do for you, Melody?" He couldn't keep the worry out of his voice.

Mel moved beneath the covers and her fingers reached for Luce. "A goodnight kiss would be wonderful, my love."

Luce grasped her outstretched hand and brushed his lips across her knuckles, not wanting to tire her out any more.

Mel laughed weakly. "Not like that. I'm not so tired that I can't tell the difference between a kiss and some archaic courtly gesture. I want a goodnight kiss where your lips mould to mine and our tongues dance between them to a song we both know and love."

"Beethoven's Ninth," Luce breathed, dropping to his knees. Mel sighed in pleasure as their lips met and Luce did his damnedest to give her a kiss with dancing in it, though a fair bit dirtier than the stately stuff of Beethoven's time.

Luce felt Mel's second sigh and her contentment, so he gently broke the kiss. Much more and he'd be in for an uncomfortable night.

"Patrick's waiting for you in the kitchen with a glass of that lovely aged whisky you boys were drinking last night. If only I wasn't so tired, I'd join you. But as it is…" She smiled. "He doesn't blame you for the shape I'm in. He knows I have a tendency to do too much. He was just shocked. If you have questions about angels or souls or anything at all, you can ask him. If I were to suggest a mentor for you, the first one I'd recommend would be Patrick. He truly does want to help you, my love."

Help him back to Hell, just like every other angel, Luce grumbled to himself but didn't dare say aloud. "I'll be back soon," he said instead, giving her one final kiss before heading back to the kitchen for the promised whisky.

Twenty-Six

To Luce's irritation, Patrick was waiting for him in the kitchen, but he was mollified by the scent of two aromatic glasses of whisky on the bench beside him.

Patrick raised his glass. "To a braver man than I am, for filling the hole in Muriel's heart."

He drank, but Luce didn't. "Why do you say that?"

"It's a brave man who'd agree to share a bond with an angel as high as Lady Muriel. I couldn't do it. I'd be terrified that one day I'd let her down, because it's inevitable that I would." He closed his eyes as he took a large sip.

Luce tasted the whisky, relishing the smooth burn as it coated the back of his throat. "Stop being evasive. Tell me what you know about angelic bonds that I don't."

Patrick nodded. "I only know what I've heard and what I've seen, as I've never been close enough to anyone to form such a powerful bond. Have you ever been bonded before? I mean, before you…became the Lord of Hell?"

Luce shook his head, gesturing for the saint to continue.

"I only ask because I've heard that demon taint is one of the ways such a bond can be severed. It's not easy, I've heard – it takes a fairly powerful angel to form or break one. Of course, it goes without saying that Mel could. But she never has. Not until now."

"She offered to dissolve it," Luce said. "If that's what I wanted."

"Did she say that's what she wanted?"

Patrick asked shrewdly.

"No. She seemed sad at the thought, to be honest. But she offered. She said she could break the bond and find me a better mentor. She suggested you." Luce drank deeply.

Patrick choked. "Me? A better mentor than Mel? I'm honoured at the compliment if she thinks so, but she's wrong. If you were to search Heaven and Earth for a better mentor than she is, good luck finding one. She's the kindest, most patient angel I've ever met and she knows more about Heaven and Earth than any angel alive. Hell, too, now, I imagine. I wish she'd offered to mentor me, but she was busy at the time and I didn't even know her then, or I'd have begged her. Instead, I worked with Uriel. He's the archangel bonded to Gabrielle, and he's been handling the situation in Russia and the Ukraine for a long time now. What I know about angelic bonds is from him."

"And that is?"

"You share everything with your partner. Every thought, feeling and emotion, even on the other side of the world. It's as if distance doesn't matter. It's a deep connection, joining two souls across some sort of dimension in space that only the most powerful angels can negotiate safely. He said that Beelzebub and Mephistopheles had had a bond like it once, before they fell, but it was broken when their souls were corrupted by darkness. Through it you feel everything. So if you ever disappoint her…you'll feel her pain as acutely as if it were your own. And Mel, well, she's heartbroken whenever she loses a soul. You'd think she'd be used to it by now, humans being as wilful as they are, but she's so incredibly optimistic that she goes into every negotiation convinced that whatever power-hungry politician she's dealing with is a paragon of virtuous, selfless leadership. And she's shattered when they demonstrate that they're as dodgy as the next bloke." He set his empty glass down. "More whisky?"

"Please." Luce waited until Patrick had finished pouring. "So you're saying I'll share her pain, but also her joy and everything else? And that she's the best mentor there is? She wants the best for me — she said so. Why would she ask me to give her up?"

Patrick's eyes stayed firmly on his drink. "She always wants the best for others. And usually she'll issue orders to that effect without giving you a choice in the matter. I've learned to trust her on things, because when she's considering the repercussions of a decision, her visions are so detailed that she doesn't miss a thing. If she offers you a choice, it means the future isn't clear to her." He winked. "And you know what that means."

Irritated, Luce slammed his glass on the counter a little more firmly than he'd intended. "No, I damn well don't. Time travel sounds like a fiction humans created. Just tell me instead of dropping maddening hints!"

Patrick shrugged. "Suit yourself. I thought you would know, but I guess you've forgotten, being a demon for so long and all. A future she can't see is one that's dependent on her decisions. She can evidently see a clear, successful future for you if you decide to leave her to pursue your angelic career with another mentor. Even one as inexperienced as me. My God, I personify everything you stood against in the Heavenly Battle. Humans with souls good enough to enter Heaven to become angels, and even rise through the choirs to outrank older, more experienced angels. If you chose me as your mentor over her, that'd be one of the most ironic pairings ever. Maybe even more unusual than you and Mel herself." Luce opened his mouth to defend Mel's choice, but closed it again as Patrick continued, "I'm sure she has her reasons and they'll be good ones, though she chooses not to share them with me. Can I offer you some advice, though?"

It was Luce's turn to shrug. "You can offer." Didn't mean he had to take any of it.

"Ask her what she wants, because to me it's pretty clear that she wants you. Breaking a bond will be even harder on her than forming one, and she wouldn't have created it lightly. Bonding isn't common and the angels who do it don't willingly break them. She's asking you to choose between promotion through the angelic choirs and an uncertain future with her. I think it's because she doesn't want to make the wrong decision for you, so it's your choice.

She's already made her preference clear: she wants you to stay with her. But she'd never force you to do it. And there's nothing more precious in this universe than her. Hell, if I were you, I'd take the bond and the beautiful mentor and count my blessings." He eyed Luce. "But if you don't want her…there are plenty of us who do."

"Sounds like sound advice, saint," Luce drawled, upending his glass to catch the last few, fiery drops on his tongue. "My thanks for the chat and the drink, but I have an angel waiting for me in bed. One I won't be letting go of before this world ends."

Patrick raised his glass in salute. "Take good care of her, devil."

Twenty-Seven

The flat smelled of bacon. Not quite Heaven, but enough to make Luce cut his shower short and head for the source of the appetising aroma.

Mel's laughter bubbled over the sizzle of what promised to be the best breakfast ever. Luce glanced around to see the source of mirth, but he only met the eyes of an equally puzzled Patrick, who shrugged.

"Good morning, sweet Melody," Luce said, moving in behind her to kiss her neck.

"Good morning, Luce, and Patrick, too," Mel responded. "Bacon's better than any alarm clock, right boys?"

"You bet." Patrick opened the fridge. "You want me to make some toast to go with that?"

Mel jerked her head at the shopping bag on the bench. "No, I picked up some fresh bakery rolls from one of the shops downstairs. I forgot how expensive food is in London. I'm used to things only costing half as much in Australia – I didn't take enough money for eggs, so I hope you don't mind."

Who needed eggs when Mel was making bacon?

"I'll make coffee, then." Patrick clicked on the kettle and rummaged through the cupboard until he pulled out the dreaded jar of instant coffee.

"NO!" Luce hadn't meant to shout so loud, but the thought of having to politely swallow instant coffee took all the pleasure out of the morning. "I'll go downstairs and buy some. I know I saw a coffee shop on the way here. Patrick, how do you take your coffee?"

Mel and Patrick both glanced at the

steaming teapot.

Luce faltered. "So neither of you want coffee?" At Mel's gentle head-shake, he stomped off to get his wallet.

"Ah, Lucifer? You might want to put some pants on," Patrick suggested. "The neighbours are likely to call the police if they see you walking down the street without any clothes." He gave a sheepish smile. "I'd bail you out, but Mel wouldn't like it if you got arrested."

Luce yanked on a pair of pants, added shoes and socks, stuffed his wallet in his pocket, and strode back to the kitchen.

"Are you sure you don't want a coffee, Mel?" Luce leaned in close, pulling her body against his.

"No, I'm fine. Really, my love." She stretched up for a kiss that he was only too happy to give. "Best be quick, though. The bacon's nearly ready."

Luce took the stairs two at a time, all the way down to the street. He dodged through the dopey office workers who evidently needed a coffee more than he did, unable to stop grinning as they stared. They'd probably never seen muscles like his in the flesh, hence why they kept their flabby bits under their buttoned-to-the-collar shirts.

He darted across the road to the first coffee shop he saw and ordered his usual to take away, which he did, five toe-tapping minutes later, along with a box of pastries that he figured he'd share with Mel.

Barely out of breath by the time he reached Patrick's building, Luce decided to take the lift so he wouldn't spill his coffee. The doors slid open and he swept across the hall to Patrick's front door and up the final flight of stairs to the flat. He arrived just in time to see Mel set two plates on the table. Patrick was squeezing some sort of sauce onto his rolls in the kitchen.

They all sat down and silence reigned until every plate was empty.

"Thank you, *Mel meum*," Patrick murmured, kissing Mel's cheek as he stood to clear the plates.

The translated Latin clicked in Luce's head: My Mel. Luce's jealousy boiled over at the sight of Mel's answering smile. "You're his?

You let him call you his?"

Patrick met his angry gaze with placid calm. "It's a pun, or play on words. *Mel* is honey in Latin, and you can't deny Mel's a sweet angel. She's as much mine as she is yours, bond notwithstanding. No man owns Lady Muriel and you'd be crazy to think you could. I don't jump down your throat when you call her Melody, though I know she can't stand the nickname. Haven't you noticed the way she winces when you say Melody Angel?"

"What?" Luce stared at Mel. "You never told me that!"

Mel's eyes dropped to the table. "I don't like being called Melody Angel. It sounds like a cartoon character and it was only meant as a joke – a name Raphael put on my resume when I applied for the job at the HELL Corporation. But the way you say Melody, your voice caressing every letter as if you wished it was my body and not just a name…I…I can't help but like it."

"I'm sorry, Mel." Patrick beat a hasty retreat to the kitchen with the dirty dishes.

"It's fine," she replied in what Luce thought

was the closest she'd ever come to lying.

Did that mean he was corrupting her, despite how impossible she said it would be? Asking her to admit her innermost desires and then taking pleasure in granting them? Or was it her exhaustion that was allowing him to taint her like this? He shouldn't…couldn't…do this to Mel.

Fine. He wouldn't call her Melody ever again.

"Say it," Mel said.

"What?"

"Go on. Say my name. The way you always have."

He fixed his eyes on her. At the slightest sign of the wincing Patrick had referred to, he'd call her nothing but Lady Muriel until the world ended. "Melody," he breathed.

She closed her eyes as her blissful smile spread wide. "I love you, Luce. And to you, I will always be your Melody." Her eyes snapped open. "But Patrick is my dearest friend. I understand that you may feel some jealousy over a friendship we've shared for more than a thousand years. Since the day I apologised to a traveller for having nothing to soften the stale bread that was all I had to share, and he said my smile was honey enough for him. You're going to have to learn to control it, like any other desire. It's part of being an angel." She nodded to Patrick, who tilted the teapot to fill her mug. "Patrick sees me sharing a bed with you every night and he's been nothing but kind to you from the moment we arrived. Tell Luce what you're hiding behind your easy grin, Patrick."

"Only for you, Mel." Patrick sprawled on the sofa with his steaming mug of tea. "I may be a saint, but when I see that bedroom door closed and I know she's chosen you over me for another night, part of me wants you to slip up and disappoint her. To revert to your old, dark ways just like you're worried you might. And then I could destroy you, put you out of your misery for breaking Mel's heart." His grin turned rueful. "I'd try to make the end as painless and quick as I could, because I wouldn't enjoy your suffering, however righteous it might be. But then I hear the joy in Mel's voice and I know you make her happy.

She's been lonely for a long time and nothing I can do will help fill that gaping hole for her, no matter how much I'd like to. And if you're what the angel I love needs to be happy, then I hope to God you have the strength to be everything she needs you to be and never disappoint her." He gulped his tea. "Now, we can all sit around and discuss our feelings and finish off with a big old sob and a hug, or I can tell you what I've found out about Mel's cousin Persephone and her adventures in Ireland."

Luce jumped to his feet. "You've been hunting that damned nephilim, too?"

Patrick waved his hand airily. "Mel called me to ask if I'd seen or spoken to Persi lately, because your personal assistant – a demon, but we won't hold that against her — seemed to think I'd been calling her at your office. It's been years since I saw or spoke to little Miss Persi, so I did some investigating. Turns out she's been visiting one of my favourite haunts – a place I found when I was still human."

Mel emerged from the kitchen with a mug in each hand. "You're a wonder, Patrick. Let's take this to the lounge room where we can be more comfortable." She carefully linked one arm through Luce's and towed him down the hall to the room where early morning sunlight streamed through the windows. Setting both mugs on the coffee table, she sank onto the sofa, gesturing for Luce to do the same. "That cup's yours, Luce. Tea, not instant coffee."

Luce nodded and took the tea as Patrick strode to an armchair. Setting his back to the sun, the saint faced them. "Story time," he said.

Twenty-eight

Mel cuddled up to his side as Luce relaxed. If Patrick could save him from having to see Persephone again, he'd give the saint all the attention he wanted.

"Right, so Mel called me, asking if Persi was here with me, because Persi had said something about me calling her. First up, I said it must have been some other bloke called Patrick. It's a popular name, after all. And when Mel said Persi was in Ireland, the odds went up. Every year hundreds of new parents here call their son Patrick. And then Mel says the girl's missing. All I had to go on was the day she arrived in Heathrow and went shopping in Omagh. And a mention of someone called Patrick."

Patrick took a sip of his tea. "I could have looked up every motorcycle club and armed IRA group in both countries, asking if they had a member called Patrick and a recently arrived, tattooed girl who called herself Persephone."

Luce snorted. It sounded like a good way for the saint to get himself killed. A plan only some Heaven-cloistered angel could come up with. No wonder Mel preferred him to the naïve saint.

"Not as crazy as it sounds. I have contacts everywhere. I could have looked them up, I said, but I didn't. She wouldn't fly halfway round the world for some biker without telling Mel. Not even Persi's that stupid."

Luce suppressed another snort. Yes, the nephilim girl was stupid enough to do anything.

"And Omagh isn't exactly the place she'd go

for that, either. So I called a friend who works security at the City of Derry Airport. And he had this funny story about a security scare a few weeks ago. It was a Ryanair flight and the baggage handlers called him because, when they were unloading the suitcases, one of them was buzzing. Standard protocol and everything, though there's usually no danger. Someone's shaver turning on. Those buttons are very sensitive, he tells me. So he and a couple of other fellows take the suitcase away from the plane and the terminal buildings, figuring they'll open it and switch the shaver off and everything will be fine. There's these three kitted-up blokes standing around a purple, glittery suitcase and one gingerly pops the lid. The buzzing gets louder, but nothing blows up, so the bloke nearest to it starts rifling through the suitcase so he can switch the bloody thing off. Anyway, he pulls out the buzzing shaver, takes one look and drops it on the tarmac. Now all three of them can see it — a vibrator with an enormous, black dildo on the end, knocked half off when it hit the ground, slapping the surface like it's spanking it.

"They just piss themselves laughing and no one knows what to do. Finally, my friend picks the thing up and switches it off, but not before he notices the dildo's got a name written down the side. Must be the model name or something – he didn't know. Anyway, this one was called Beelzebub.

"Now, standard procedure is that they have to check through the luggage for any other dangerous devices, so the third bloke who hasn't gotten his hands on Beelzebub's vibrator draws the short straw and it's his turn. He finds a case hidden under all the shoes and it's full of…oh Hell, you'll never guess. More of the things, all different shapes and sizes, each with a demon name on it. Satan, Pluto, Mephistopheles…and one weird-looking thing the bloke told me he found out was something you put up your arse. I mean, who sticks things up their arse? That one was the littlest, he said, and the tiny letters on it said it was called Lucifer."

Mel smothered her laughter. "Oh, my love, I'm sorry, but you have to admit it's funny."

Lucifer the butt plug. Funny as Hell. He wasn't laughing. Right now, he'd like to shove all of Persi's toys up her back passage at the same time and see how she liked being tormented.

"Anyway, after finding nothing more dangerous than sex toys and stilettos, they had to pack the whole thing back up again and take it into the terminal. My friend was curious, wondering what sort of girl would need all that equipment, so he volunteered. And when he got to the luggage counter, there's this skinny little brunette in a skirt that barely covers her backside, and boots on stilts, bemoaning the loss of her luggage. So when he gets there with the glittery purple thing, the girl squeals and throws herself at my friend. She's kissing him and he's trying to push her away, because he has a wife and kids and the last thing he needs is her purple lipstick on his shirt collar for the rest of the work day or when he gets home, and he sees the attendant at the luggage desk choking. So he manages to peel the crazy suitcase girl off him and goes to help the other woman. Turns out she's choking because when the girl was trying to climb him like some sort of crazed monkey, the woman saw the girl had nothing but a tattoo under her skirt. He said it was like a painting on a church ceiling, except on her arse. What a place to put it, eh?"

Luce thought he was going to be physically sick all over Patrick's timber floors. Just the thought of the nephilim's Hellish tattoo was enough to make him lose his bacon sandwiches.

"It's all right, my love," Mel soothed. The nausea disappeared under her stroking fingers. She sighed. "Yes, that sounds like Persi."

Luce could feel Patrick's eyes on him but he didn't look up. He kept his gaze on Mel's hands. It was one thing to admit weakness to her, another entirely to let some saint see it.

"Why are you looking for her, anyway?" Patrick asked. "Shouldn't you delegate that to Raphael or someone else who can do the legwork? Surely you have better things to do."

Mel swallowed. "She's disappeared, but before she did…she made Luce's life a living Hell. As his PA, she messed up every task he gave her until I made her call me from wherever they were, every day, to make sure she did her job. She developed an unhealthy obsession for poor Luce where she demanded he sleep with her, despite his frequent refusals."

Please don't mention the time I gave in to temptation and let her touch me, Luce prayed. He'd had flashbacks that ended with her biting it off.

Mel's hand squeezed his. "When I…when Luce and I first bonded, she came after him again. Spread lies to her mother and Michael and Raphael, saying he'd done things that he hadn't. She even tried to keep him out of Heaven. When he retreated into Hell instead, she followed him. I don't know how. We all know no angel's been far into Hell and come out the same…well, except me, of course." She laughed shakily. "But she tormented him in his lair. Turned up at odd times and entered the place when no one else could. And then she just disappeared. Raphael can't get hold of her and he was desperate enough to ask for my help, because he knows that Persi will always see me, no matter what she's done." Mel's voice dropped lower. "And I need to see her. To make her leave Luce alone. I should never have agreed to let her take over my position, so I bear some of the responsibility for her mistakes."

"The Hell you do!" Luce growled. "That nephilim bitch wasn't obeying your orders when she was taunting me in Hell, telling me you'd never love someone like me, or telling tales of rape to any angel who'd listen. Lying through her damn teeth!"

After a few moments' silence, Patrick cleared his throat. "Ah, okay." More silence, followed by, "Do you want to hear the rest of this? Or should I just give you the rough summary?"

"I'd like to hear the rest, please," Mel said softly. "But…could you leave out the descriptions of Persi? We all know what she looks like."

"Sure." Patrick nodded and continued, "Anyway, she dragged her luggage over to the hire car desk and he didn't see her again. That's all my friend told me. Now, it's only an hour or so's drive from there to Omagh, so I figured I needed to go to Asda, too. I wandered around, grabbed a few things, and then went up the sweets aisle. The Toffee Crisps were on special and I remember you saying they don't have those things in Australia, so I thought I'd see if I could get a box for you to take home, because I know how much you like them. There were only a couple left on the shelf, so I asked one of the staff if they had a box out in the storeroom. The girl laughed and asked me if I was going to Purgatory, too."

Mel nodded knowingly, but Luce was lost. "You need chocolate to bribe your way into Purgatory?"

"She was talking about St Patrick's Purgatory," Patrick explained, which left Luce more confused than ever. Before he could demand more explanation, Patrick went on. "The Sanctuary of St Patrick is an old monastery on Station Island in Loch Dearg in Ireland. About half an hour's drive from Omagh, a few miles past the border. I remember it as a remote island in the middle of the lake. I'd take a *curach* — ah, that's a little boat — out there, where I'd live in a cave and catch fish in the lake. I only did it once when I was alive, but when I returned here on Mel's orders it became a regular retreat. Mel called it a sabbatical and said I was entitled to it, much as she was to hers, but it truly was just a holiday. I thought it was my secret, but a local farmer spotted me sitting in front of a campfire, cooking my catch, and hopped in his own little boat for a look-see. When I returned a few years later, there were stories in the local village about how the apparition of St Patrick had been seen on the island, praying to protect them from the fires of Hell in the cave. My island had a dozen pilgrims on it, making a Hell of a racket, loudly praying for a visitation of their own. Their Latin was terrible. I must have made some comment about it being Hell and Purgatory for the poor saint, seeing as I couldn't sleep a wink that trip. Centuries later, someone got it into his head to build a monastery on the spot to plug the hole to Hell and it's been slowly expanding ever since. The monastery, not the hole. They probably filled the cave in when they built over the top of it.

"With Mel's permission, I visit the place

every year if I can. But I had to promise no miracles." Patrick laughed. "Anyway, now the place is called St Patrick's Purgatory or the Sanctuary of St Patrick, though it's a far cry from the little slice of Heaven I had all to myself all those years ago. And once with Mel."

Mel burst out laughing. "That's the first time you've ever referred to that trip in the same breath as Heaven. I still remember that storm. I said I wished I had a cup of milk to help me sleep so I wouldn't keep waking up with every roll of thunder. You dragged your boat out to the lake and insisted you'd be back with my milk." She glanced at Luce. "You know what he did? Two hours later, he returned with a goat. A live nanny goat. I don't know what he traded for her, but it cost us most of our clothing before we left the island and returned her to the farmer Patrick had bought her off. She ate everything we weren't wearing and then she'd start nibbling on my skirt when I wasn't looking. I tried tying her up with my last spare stocking and she ate that too!"

"I'd forgotten about the goat," Patrick

admitted.

Luce fought down the jealous demon trying to claw its way out of his gut. He needed to take Mel on a holiday with just the two of them, he decided. One where they could have hilarious hijinks with farm animals. He could be the hero who persuaded Mel to slip her stockings off to use as restraints. No goat necessary…

"I know that look, my love, and I'd love to know what's inspiring it. Later," Mel murmured in Luce's ear, pausing to kiss his cheek before she raised her voice. "Sorry, Patrick. Now Luce is up to speed on why there's a monastery named after you, can we continue with what you've found out about Persi?"

"Sure," Patrick replied. He tilted his mug, but it was empty. "Can we take a quick tea break? I might have some biscuits somewhere."

"I bought some cakes with my coffee," Luce offered. "There should be enough for all of us to share." He glanced down in surprise to find he'd finished his tea, too.

Patrick took the empty mugs to the kitchen, promising he'd return with tea and cakes to continue the story.

Luce wasn't fussed. Mel was a warm weight beside him and he was happy just to be with her. To Hell with nephilim, goats and monasteries.

Twenty-nine

Patrick's polite cough intruded and Mel ended the passionate kiss, to Luce's chagrin. "Later," she whispered before turning her attention to the platter in Patrick's hands. "Ooh, an almond croissant. Can I take it? Do you mind?" She looked from Patrick to Luce as her hand hovered over the pastry.

Both men shrugged in synchrony. There was no way Luce would deny her the pleasure of eating her treat, or himself the pleasure of watching her as she enjoyed herself.

"Oh, for Heaven's sake." Mel seized the croissant and bit into it, closing her eyes as she hummed happily. After she swallowed, she said, "There is nothing erotic about me eating cake." She took an exaggeratedly large bite and Patrick turned red. Luce just chuckled.

Patrick coughed. "There's…um, there's a couple of Toffee Crisps, too." He pointed at the orange-wrapped chocolate bars Luce hadn't noticed until now. "The shop assistant found a box for me and it's in the kitchen. Make sure I remember to give it to you before you leave."

Mel swallowed the last of her croissant. "You're wonderful. Thank you, Patrick." She snagged both bars from the table and offered one to Luce, who shook his head. She tossed it back, set the second one on the arm of the couch and reached for her tea. "Now can we please go back to Purgatory? Or Asda."

"Right. Asda. The bars. Well, it was odd that the girl at the supermarket mentioned Purgatory, so I asked her whether she got many pilgrims. She said they didn't, except when they were lost, like the strange foreign girl a few weeks ago. This girl came in and loaded a trolley up with all the Toffee Crisps they had, insisting she needed them to take with her. She said she was going to Loch Dearg and she needed directions because she was lost. The shop assistant…her name was Orlaith. Very traditional name. And she looked like one, too. She was very helpful and showed Persi where to go, then asked why the girl needed so many. After all, it was only a three-day retreat – she could come back on the way home. Persi said something about a gift for her cousin in Australia." Patrick grinned. "What a coincidence, huh?"

Luce snorted. "Luck, surely."

"Angels' luck," Mel said softly. "When it's not for personal gain, everything goes right. It's what won me the HELL Corporation coffee machine, Luce. But it doesn't answer the question of where Persi is. Three weeks ago, she bought me a box of chocolate bars, but she hasn't come home to deliver it. So where is she?" Plastic crackled as she unwrapped a bar and bit into it. "Mmm."

Patrick and Luce sat in silence, just watching

her. Luce's mind spun through the possibilities of Mel, some warm chocolate and all the pleasurable noises she could make. One day he'd try to persuade her to try…

Without opening her eyes, Mel said, "Me eating chocolate isn't erotic, either. This is getting silly." She held the bar out to Luce. "Here, you try some. If you'd gone for years without one, wouldn't you be savouring the taste and texture just a bit, too?"

Unable to refuse, Luce took a bite, crunching through the gritty, gooey aggregate of caramel, biscuit and chocolate. Sure it was sweet, but nowhere near as sweet as the thought of licking warm chocolate off Mel's bare skin. Maybe she'd even be willing to reciprocate.

The crackling of plastic brought him out of his daydream as Mel dropped the empty wrapper on the coffee table. "That's the last time I eat a chocolate bar in front of you boys. Thank you again, Patrick, but…"

Patrick laughed. "Ah, you're irresistible when you're enjoying yourself. You just don't do it enough, *Mel meum*."

Luce agreed. "As soon as we sort out this

mess with the nephilim, we're going to change that, Melody."

Mel inclined her head. "You're both very sweet, but there's still Persi to find. So where was she, Patrick? Purgatory?"

"She was," Patrick replied. "I spoke to the prior and he definitely remembers her. A snippy little thing, swearing about getting stuck in a flock of sheep on one of the roads. He thought she was going to stab him with one of her spiky heels when he suggested she take her shoes off, she was so angry. She snapped that she wasn't one of his pilgrims — she was looking for Patrick's place. She raged and swore a bit, saying I went there every year and she wanted to see my place. Of course, the prior doesn't know who I really am — though he knows me as a regular visitor. So he told Persi that I'd already done my pilgrimage this year but he'd be happy to help her with hers. He gave her a map of the grounds and sent her off. As the day progressed, he heard an increasing number of complaints from pilgrims about a loud, foul-mouthed girl in high heels who seemed to have traversed the whole island

and every building on it, upsetting everyone as she went. When the last boat of the day left the island, she was on it."

Luce snorted. "I'd have kicked her off the island, too. Not exactly the sort of person to help with religious contemplation or whatever people do there."

"No, he didn't have to. She left of her own volition, he said. Whatever she was looking for, she hadn't found it and she departed in high dudgeon. Apparently, she broke one of her heels, so she'd spent most of her day barefoot, too." Patrick laughed. "Seems angelic luck doesn't apply to little Miss Persi. The prior said her eyes seemed almost red by evening, as if she was possessed."

"But demons can't possess an immortal's constructed body," Mel objected. "If Persi left it for a day, it'd disintegrate into dust. Perhaps he imagined it."

"I saw her eyes flash red, too, when she came after me in Hell," Luce offered. "She had to get in there somehow. I figured it was the power I signed over to her that did it."

Mel shook her head. "No. You can't sign

over Hell – just your corporation and all your Earthly possessions. Your soul, too, if it came down to it. But to relinquish your responsibilities in Hell itself, you'd have to speak to your angelic superior to be relieved of your duties, and a replacement would need to be found. But not Persi. Persi will never be the ruler of Hell."

"I don't think one of your superior angels would care about whether she's a good choice or not. None of the higher angels like me and they'd happily take power off me if they could, especially if they could replace me with someone as submissive as that nephilim." Luce leaned forward. "Not all angels are as practical as you, Mel."

Patrick burst out laughing and even Mel managed a small smile.

Luce got the impression he'd said something stupid. "Okay, what's funny?"

Patrick pointed at Mel. "She's your superior and the one who picks your replacement. The Domination of Heaven, Earth and Hell. If Mel says Persi will never rule Hell, then she won't. But that doesn't explain the red eyes. A tainted or demonic soul does that. Is it possible that Persi…Persi herself is a demon?" The tightening worry lines around his eyes betrayed his pain at the possibility.

Silence reigned for a few seconds, through which Luce could faintly hear the traffic downstairs. He shifted uncomfortably. No one had mentioned what he'd done to the girl yet, but it was only a matter of time. Better to admit it than wait for Mel to reveal the truth.

"I did give her the dark souls that shrouded mine," he said. "If she welcomed them into her soul, she could be a demon."

"Summon her, then," Patrick said, taking a biscuit from the dwindling tray of cakes. "If she's a demon, then the Lord of Hell can summon her to do his bidding." He returned Mel and Luce's stares. "What? It beats you two haring around after her. And if you can't summon her, then she's not a demon."

"Yet," Mel said softly. She gripped Luce's arm. "Do it please, my love. If Persi's a demon, I need to know. Maybe I can help her. The sooner we find her, the better."

Thirty

"Summon a demon? Don't we need a witch for that? You know, with spells and candles and herbs and animal entrails?" Luce laughed shakily. "You know that stuff rarely works for humans, unless there's a mischievous imp around. If Persephone's turned into a demon, then she chose her fate. Not even you can help her if that's what she wants, Mel."

"I helped you," she said. "Please, Luce. Even as a demon, she'll still speak to me."

He couldn't refuse her. "Fine. If you want

her here, I'll summon her. But if she is a demon, I want to send her to Hell where she'll stay out of my way. I don't like her and the more I see her, the greater the temptation to snap her neck."

Closing his eyes, Luce concentrated on the nephilim as he'd last seen her in his lair in Hell. Dressed in an ankle-length dress that didn't tempt him in the slightest and with red, flashing eyes that had put him off more than her Hellish tattoo had. He wanted her here, now, to answer to him and Mel why she'd left the HELL Corporation and all her responsibilities, giving Raphael an excuse to try and order him around, and breaking up his first Heavenly idyll with Mel. She'd fit right in with Lilith and the other harpies in Level Seven.

He wanted her skinny arse here so he could banish her back to Hell. Right now.

Luce squinted at the rug, where he'd focussed his energy. It was mercifully nephilim-free. His breath hissed through his teeth. "She's not a demon. I can't summon her."

He felt Mel relax in his arms. "Oh, thank God. But if she could become one, we need to find her. I can't let that happen, Luce. I just can't." She lifted teary eyes to Patrick. "Did your prior friend say anything about where Persi was headed or even why she was looking for you?"

Patrick shook his head. "Nope. If she'd wanted to find me, all she'd have to do is look me up. Patrick Driscoll, political adviser, isn't a hard man to track down when my number's listed on the consultancy website. She's not after me, *Mel meum*. She's searching for something else. Something she didn't find at Loch Dearg."

"But what? Why would she disappear without leaving word for me, or even asking for my help? Persi never does anything without consulting me. Why now?" Mel looked troubled.

"Can't you look into the future and find out?" Patrick ventured.

Mel shook her head. "No. Whatever she's doing has rendered Persi's future dark to me. Which means it must have something to do with me, but I don't see how."

Or me, Luce thought darkly. Mel's future was intimately entwined with his and he wouldn't let her go lightly, so whatever trouble Persephone intended to bring to Mel's door, he'd be the one answering her knock. Being a nuisance in his life and domain was bad enough. Disrupting Mel's life when she needed rest? Unacceptable.

"Hey, go easy on the furniture, Lucifer. If you want to take your frustration out on anything, I know a couple of concrete eyesores in London that could benefit from demolition. Probably best if you wait until dark, though."

Luce pried his fingers off the sofa arm, surreptitiously trying to fill the gouges in the wood. "I could do with blowing off a little steam," he admitted.

"Not destroying buildings," Mel objected. "Surely there's something that'll draw less attention than that."

"Well, we could head up to the pub tonight. You, me and the devil." Patrick grinned. "It's been your favourite for centuries and it's still open. The new management has made some changes that I think you might like, Mel."

"Pub tonight then. Sounds like a plan," Luce said, stretching. "Anything that doesn't involve that nuisance nephilim sounds great to me."

Thirty-one

"It's green," Luce observed, staring at the pub. "Matches your sweater, Patrick."

"It's a jumper. Got to speak the language or people won't understand you," Patrick replied. "Who cares as long as the beer's not green? Though on my name day, it usually is." He led the way through the worn wooden doors that Mel knew well.

"After you," Luce said with an elaborate bow.

Mel blushed, smiled and followed Patrick.

She felt Luce's hands grasp her hips.

"Hell, you look sexy in jeans. The way the denim clings to your curves as if it was made for you. Are you sure you don't want to go straight home and help me get you out of them?"

She laughed merrily. "No, Luce. You need to blow off some steam and I admit I'd like to see you in action on the dance floor. From what I remember, this place has a good one."

"Ooh, it's good to see you back, Mr Driscoll," the girl at the entry desk said. "I've missed your accent. Just you, as always?"

Patrick grinned. "I brought some friends from Australia with me tonight, so it'll be three." He gestured at Mel and Luce, then offered his wrist for the girl to stamp.

"I hope you've been practising for tonight," the girl bubbled, inking a blurry birdcage on Mel's wrist.

"Oh, I'm more than good enough. I've had all the practice I'll ever need," Luce drawled, winking at the girl as he extended his hand for a stamp.

She giggled. "Someone's very confident.

Good luck with the competition, then."

Competition? Mel wanted to ask, but Patrick urged them to hurry and Luce pulled her with him.

Patrick headed for the bar, shouting at them to get a table near the stage. As they approached, a group rose together and headed out of the pub, leaving one of the bar staff to collect the glasses and give the table a cursory wipe. Front and centre – perfect. Luce helped Mel before taking the chair beside her.

Luce picked up one of the menus on the table and leafed through it, then threw it down. "It's not a drinks menu, it's a music one. Seems they take their dancing very seriously here."

"Dancing? Hell no. Friday nights are for karaoke. With all the choir practice you two get, I figure I'll have some stiff competition tonight." Patrick set three pints of beer on the table and plonked himself on a chair opposite Luce. "I had you pegged for Miley Cyrus' *Wrecking Ball*, Lucifer. What do you think?"

Luce swallowed his mouthful of beer. "I think I can do better than that."

Patrick pushed Mel's beer across the table to

her. "What about you, Mel?"

Her insides froze. Singing in public? If there was anything worse than public speaking, it was singing. And she couldn't sing. She'd be lucky to emit a squeak. "I'll just enjoy my beer and the show, I think," she said, trying to stop her hands from shaking as she lifted her pint. Some of it slopped onto the table and she sighed.

"A saint versus the devil? I like those odds. Care for a wager on the result, Patrick?" Luce asked. He scrawled a song choice on his paper and covered it before Mel could read it.

Patrick shrugged. "Sure. Loser pays for the last round of drinks and the cab home. And Mel can judge."

"You're on." Luce shoved back from the table and headed for the DJ booth to hand over his selection slip. He winked at Mel as he returned, slipping an arm around her shoulders as he lifted his beer in his other hand.

By the time they'd finished their first pints, the pub was more than half full and Luce had to wait at the bar for several minutes before he returned with their second round of drinks.

"Looks like they're about to start," he said, nodding at the stage and a costumed Elvis impersonator.

The MC opened with an explanation of how karaoke worked and the rules of the competition. Even Mel tuned out a little before the end; but then again, the rules didn't apply to her. She definitely wouldn't be singing.

She clapped and cheered politely for the first few acts, feeling that the performers' courage deserved her applause even if their performance didn't. After all, who was she to criticise them for being brave enough to do what she couldn't?

Before she knew it, Patrick jumped to his feet. "That's me!" he shouted, jogging up the steps to the stage.

He got a healthy cheer from the audience, which made Mel wonder just how many times Patrick came here. He winked at her and launched into U2's *Beautiful Day*. He played to the crowd and not just her. The way he spread his arms and raised his eyes Heavenward for each chorus made her almost expect the ceiling to open up and let a blaze of light in. She knew he could do it, too.

Mel applauded until her hands tingled when he was done, and again when a beaming Patrick thumped into his seat. He drained his beer in one long pull, slamming it down on the table before heading for the next round. Both Luce and Patrick had made it clear that she wouldn't be buying – not when they were engaged in some sort of chivalric competition for her.

She almost choked on her beer when the MC announced, "Next up…Lucifer, who's *Bad to the Bone!*"

Luce released her hand and grinned as he ran his fingers through his hair. Was that…a horn? Two? They were hidden again before Mel could be sure, but surely Luce wouldn't…not if he'd given his real name! She grabbed Patrick's arm. "He's going up there as himself in front of what must be more than a hundred people! What if he breaks out his wings?"

Patrick just laughed. "Even if he did, this mob would probably just laugh and cheer louder. Costumes are normal here. Didn't you see Elvis? No one will believe he's really Lucifer, and they'll love the character they think he is."

Luce had left his jacket draped over the back of his chair, so he loosened the first couple of shirt buttons to expose his sculpted pectoral muscles. His growled imitation of George Thorogood was so good it was bad...or bad that it was good? It vibrated through her bones like powerful bass. By the first chorus, all his shirt buttons were history and he'd whipped it off, whirling it above his head as if he wanted to lasso himself a girl from the crowd. Instead, he tossed the shirt on the table in front of Mel, to riotous screams from what sounded like every girl in the pub.

"Impress me," she whispered, knowing he could hear her.

He grinned at her over the guitar solo and caressed his rippled abdominal muscles. The screaming increased in volume.

When Luce reached the second chorus, Mel clapped her hands over her mouth. Luce's tail poked out of the back of his pants and it was writhing and lashing in perfect rhythm to his song – no way in Hell would they believe it wasn't real!

Screams and cheers greeted his devilish appearance as he ran his fingers through his hair to reveal his horns. Every gyration of his hips, wink or blown kiss seemed directed at her – was he playing the crowd, or was he truly focussing his devilishly sexy performance solely on her?

He finished with a slide across the floor on his knees to her side, chest thrust out and slick with sweat from what had been a very energetic performance. The last notes of the song died away as he jumped up, grabbed her and planted a passionate kiss on her lips.

Panting, Luce seemed oblivious to the deafening cheer that erupted around them. His exhilarated eyes drank her in – Mel could feel the love fizzing through him.

"Well, I guess the devil has to win occasionally," Patrick said, sighing as he headed to the bar for more beer.

Thirty-two

"Mel, singing *Angel!*" the MC shouted, startling Mel.

She laughed shakily. "For a minute, I thought he meant me."

Patrick was grinning. "Of course he does. When you were too shy to put in a request, I made one for you. You'll be great, Mel. Go on." He stood up and hauled Mel to her feet. "She's here!" he shouted.

Her knees liquefied as her insides froze. No. She couldn't. She couldn't go up on stage.

Luce's arms around her kept her upright.

"It'll be all right, Melody. I'll help you."

"Luce, I'm not singing," she insisted.

"You don't have to. Just sit there and look angelic and I'll do all the work." He winked as he hauled a chair onto the stage, then lifted her up after it. He grabbed the microphone. "Mel's a little shy, so I'll help her out or we'll spend all our time waiting." Laughter and cheers followed.

Mel pressed her denim-clad knees together, willing them to stop shaking. No one was staring at her – it was Luce capturing all their attention. Her blood ran cold as the MC nodded to them. She closed her eyes as the opening notes of the Sarah McLachlan song rang out, but couldn't help smiling as Luce changed the words to leave everyone in no doubt that the broken man in the song was him. Every line was "I" and "me" and "my" – and as his voice soared effortlessly into the chorus, he made it clear that his angel was her.

Tears cascaded down her cheeks as she opened her eyes to the realisation that this was no performance. How could he bear to lay himself bare in front of hundreds of people? It didn't seem to matter how many people were watching – raw emotion radiated off him, engulfing her in its potency. Even Luce succumbed to the power of it, falling to his knees at the end of the second verse to wrap his arms around her as he delivered the chorus one more time.

He rose at the end of it, gathering her into his arms as he repeated the last two lines, but this time it was his angel in his arms and it was Heaven he wanted her to find there. He carried her down the steps back to their table, paying no attention to the cheering crowd.

Under the cover of the next contestant's spirited rendition of Nancy Sinatra's infamous boots, Luce leaned across the table to snarl at Patrick, "What in Hell were you thinking? You could have asked her before you put her through an ordeal like that! She's terrified of public speaking – and singing's one step further. Did you think a phobia like that would just vanish with a couple of beers?"

No. Patrick had had no idea what her greatest fear was, as he'd never seen her in a situation where she'd been forced to reveal it until now.

He quailed, turning terrified eyes on Mel. "I didn't know. Mel, I swear I didn't know. I thought you were just a bit nervous like most people are. I had no idea it ran deeper than that. You're so confident in everything else, I never thought that…"

Mel summoned a queasy smile. "It's all right," she began.

"No it isn't!" Luce interrupted. "You have the gall to have a go at me for not taking care of her and yet you do something bloody stupid like this. You're as much of a hypocrite as every other angel."

Mel grabbed his arm and yanked him down. "Luce, he didn't know. He didn't know. I never told him."

Patrick shoved back from the table. "I'll go get another round. Mel, d'you want another one?" He waved at her half-full glass.

"Just water, please," she said, not letting go of Luce until Patrick had vanished into the crowd.

"They think they're so perfect," Luce muttered. He eyed her beer. "Are you going to drink that?" When she shook her head, her half-pint disappeared down his throat.

"Patrick isn't perfect and he made a mistake that he apologised for. I understand that you're angry, Luce, but you can't blame him for not knowing. It's not something I like sharing. You only found out because…well, the lobsters. And then that awful presentation a few weeks ago. Hell, Luce, the whole point of tonight was to blow off some steam, not build up a new head of pressure. Just…let it go, please. You turned his mistake into a memory I'll treasure 'til the world ends. Please don't taint it. You have a magnificent singing voice and your performance is…mesmerising. Both as my sexy devil and a redeemed one."

Luce seemed to relax a little. He nodded slowly, but his expression didn't lighten. "I'll be right back," he said, slipping away.

Mel's gaze followed him through the crowd until she was certain he was headed in the opposite direction to the way Patrick had gone. She sighed and slumped in her seat. So much for a relaxing night. She rubbed her temples, trying to soothe away her worries. It felt like there was a storm brewing in her head. The sound of glasses clinking surprised her into opening her eyes.

"I brought your water, beer for us blokes and one of those fruit juice cocktails you liked so much in Sri Lanka. One with no alcohol, I swear." Patrick pointed at the obscenely pink pint glass between the golden ones. "Where's your devil gone?"

Mel shrugged and sniffed the pink concoction. "Little boys' room, perhaps. He didn't say."

"Well, these will have to be our last drinks. Last song, too. They're getting close to closing time." Patrick's eyes widened. "Oh, Mel, he's not in the loos at all. I think he's been bitten by the karaoke bug."

Mel followed his gaze to the stage. With his horns and tail out, Luce had somehow acquired an old-fashioned shirt, tailcoat and top hat. Luce caught her eye, grinned and swept off his hat as Mel recognised the opening bars of The Rolling Stones' *Sympathy for the Devil*.

She didn't know how he did it. With every

bum-wiggle, thrust of his hips or wink, he had girls screaming his name. The lyrics only had him egging them on, detailing what she knew were only a tiny taste of his many sins, yet they loved him for it.

Off came the hat, then the coat, and the shirt soon followed, though he tossed them to the MC instead of into the crowd or at her. When he was down to just his pants, he hooked his thumbs into the waistband and grinned at Mel.

She shook her head and mouthed an emphatic NO that he met with a wink, which sent the girl at the table behind Mel into hysterics. Mel remained resolute and it took him several seconds of tugging at his mysteriously jammed zipper before he gave up and kept his pants on, making up for their presence with even more erotic dance moves.

Luce's gyrations ceased as the music died away and he jumped off the stage to return to the table. He emptied his beer in three gulps, then wiped his mouth with the back of his hand.

"I think I should take you home before

someone else tries to," Mel murmured, jerking her head at the scrum of girls fighting their way from the foot of the stairs to their table.

Luce nodded and shrugged on his jacket, curling a possessive arm around Mel as they followed Patrick into the cool air outside.

A surprisingly smooth cab ride through the dark London streets ended at Patrick's flat. He followed Mel and Luce into the lift, mourning his upstaging. "Every time I go there now, all they'll remember is that I was the one who brought Lucifer, the man who stole the show." He shook his head sadly. "How was I to know you'd learned to be a secret rock star in your time on Earth?"

"You've forgotten your theology, saint," Luce said. "If you'd remembered, you'd know that I was a choirmaster in the Seraphim, one of the highest choirs of angels that did nothing but weave melodies for millennia. I used to conduct symphonies so complex they were outside the realms of human perception, long before humans were allowed into Heaven. And Melody…she'd inspire any man to sing." He tried to kiss her hand but missed. He managed on the third try. "Damn, I'm drunk."

Thirty-three

"I haven't been this drunk since the sixties. Hell, I was in London then, too. Hasn't changed much. Still so bloody dull that you need to drink to keep sane." Luce stumbled out of the lift and leaned against a wall while they waited for Patrick to unlock the door.

"What were you doing in London? The 1960s, you mean, or an earlier century?" Mel asked, her hands braced behind Luce's back to ensure he only headed up the stairs without falling down them.

"Yes, the last ones. The ones where there were plenty of musicians who wanted to make it big and they'd sign over their souls for fame, fortune and immortality. We couldn't create the contracts fast enough – it was incredible. I tossed back a few drinks while I was waiting for the band to finish their set, and they seemed popular enough to get asked for a few encores, so I drank a few more. The place was packed and I fell to talking to a couple of other guys who said they were friends of the band. Turned out they had a band of their own, but it was more of a loose arrangement, jamming with whoever they could at their occasional gigs. One bloke's name was Keith and I think the other's name was Michael or something. Or were they the guys in the band who were playing? Don't remember. I was that pissed." Luce lurched around to grin at Mel. "Like now. You know I love you, don't you, Mel? Mel. Melody. Melody my sweet, sweet angel."

"Yes, I do. I love you too, Luce. But I'm not sure you should be telling me about buying musicians' souls. That's the past, not the present, my love." She grabbed him before he swayed back down the stairs.

"No, didn't buy them. It was all in the contracts. They wanted stuff and that's what they were willing to offer. But not these two. Uh-uh." Luce grinned. "The more they drank, the more they told me about the woes of being a musician. So when they were as drunk as I was, I told them the Hell of being a musician was nothing compared to being the eternal Lord of Hell. The things I'd had to do to win souls, the things I'd seen humans do to each other, and how damn rude humans could be when they didn't want what I was offering. Or when they did and they didn't have the guts to admit it. As if the haughty humans were better than me. All I wanted was a bit of sympathy. And courtesy. And Meith and Kichael agreed with me! Couple of good blokes, really. One piped up that it gave him an idea for a song and he asked for some of my spare paper to write on. Contracts for their souls and they wanted to write on the back of them. I just laughed and let them, then took the papers home." Luce stumbled up the last step into Patrick's living room. "I didn't see them properly until the next morning. They'd scribbled all over those contracts, signed their names at the bottom and all, but not on the line where it was supposed to be. Hell no. At the bottom of what looked like song lyrics on the back of the contract. Damn poetry about being the devil. Good poetry, though. And I thought to myself, if they ever turn it into a half-decent song, I'd take that over their souls. Who needs a couple more mediocre musicians in Hell, anyway?" He collapsed on the sofa, humming the Stones song loudly.

Patrick pulled Mel into the kitchen and poured her a pint glass of water. "What is he babbling about? Did he just tell you he bought Keith Richards' and Mick Jagger's souls for a song?"

Mel sipped the water and smiled. "No. I mean, he might've tried – he's Lucifer, and there's no telling what he got up to when he was a demon – but you don't believe the devil would be so sentimental as to take a song over a soul?"

Patrick shrugged. "He sought redemption and signed over everything for the angel he loves, Mel. He even serenaded you in front of a whole pub full of strangers. He's plenty sentimental, all right."

She peeped around the corner. Lucifer was still stretched out on the couch, but humming had given way to snoring. "And he's passed out, too."

"Want to go into the lounge so we can let him sleep?"

Mel nodded silently, so Patrick grabbed the jug of filtered water and they headed for the lounge room. The moon shone through the casement windows, turning the warm-coloured room into stark shades of white, black and grey. Leached of colour, it felt cold.

Patrick clicked on the light and Mel reached for a golden-brown throw rug, wrapping it around her shoulders like a shawl. She sank into an armchair and pulled her knees up to her chest. Patrick sprawled across the sofa, propping his head up on a cushion so she could see his face.

"Did you have fun tonight?" he asked, starting intently at her.

"Yes."

"So explain to me why Lucifer was shouting at me for ruining your night."

Mel sighed, reminding herself that Patrick knew she wasn't perfect. It was still hard to admit to something so silly, though. "I suffer from glossophobia – I'm terrified of public speaking. Around three thousand years ago, I helped a Cretan king judge the guilt of his people when they were accused of crimes. When I proclaimed a woman's innocence, the king shouted that I was a liar. He'd set up the girl to take the fall instead of the real culprit, and he had the whole crowd convinced she was guilty. So he handed me and the innocent woman to a mob. An unarmed mob, but it didn't matter. There were so many of them, they tore us apart with their bare hands. It was a slow and very traumatic death. To this day, I'm reminded of that mob every time I speak to a group of people, or if I'm the centre of attention. My knees turn to jelly, my insides to ice and my tongue to stone. I can't speak and I can barely stand."

Patrick's expression shifted from anger to horror to pity. "And you never told me."

"No. You didn't need to know. No one did. I resolved then to only help with advice or as an individual needs me – I don't stand in judgement over humans. Never again."

His eyes narrowed. "Yet Lucifer knew."

Mel squeezed her eyes shut. "Yes. He…oh, take my hand. It's easier to both show and tell you." She fluttered her fingers at Patrick and his hands were warm and smooth as he clasped hers between them. The memory surfaced, as bright and clear as the day it happened, and she softly narrated, "There was a press conference at the HELL Corporation and I was sent to brief Luce with some essential, additional information. When I walked in, everyone turned to me – microphones, cameras, yammering faces…my knees buckled. And Luce…he helped me up and he held on to me until he dismissed the reporters. When we were alone, he asked if there was anything more he could do or if I'd be all right. He just knew and I didn't have to tell him."

Patrick's smile looked forced. "Good thing he wasn't a demon any more, then, or he'd have thrown you to the wolves. Instead, he turned you into a heroine."

"Oh, he was a demon, all right. It was just after I got back from Sri Lanka and he saw the photos. He said some strange things, too – that I'd saved him twice already. I don't think either of us expected I'd do it again." Mel managed a small smile. "At the time, I expected him to take advantage of my weakness somehow and use it against me, but he never did. At Heaven's gates, so many people came to see his triumphal re-entry. I dressed up – all in gold, wings out to their fullest extent, practically glowing – and all those angels were staring at me. Then Peter said something about how I'd saved Lucifer and conquered Hell and he bowed. And that's how it works – the name, the full glory and all of a sudden I've gone from the Melody Angel, a nameless angel who's nothing special, to Lady Muriel, one of the highest in Heaven, and everyone has to bow and scrape and obey and…oh, the worst part…pay attention to me. What kind of leader can't bear to give orders to their followers, Patrick?" She laughed nervously. "Truth is, the prophesied threat of Lucifer dragging me into Hell was only an excuse for me hiding on Earth all these centuries. If everyone knew me, I'd have to take on more authority and address more people and…all those things I can't stand. Instead, I've delegated to Raphael and let him be my spokesangel. It worked pretty well most of the time, except when it came to Luce. I've spent so long being invisible that Raphael seemed to think I needed to be."

Patrick laughed. "Oh, I could have told him he had nothing to worry about. You're not easily tempted."

The silence hung between them, filled with unsaid declarations of love that Patrick had never voiced. And never would.

"I'm sorry I'll never be powerful enough to support you like he can. A born angel and one of the highest at that – he's what you deserve. Your equal, which I'll never be. I was raised to adulthood as a slave and even after all this time, it still shows."

"Patrick. You were the first human to become a Hashmallim. Don't underestimate your own worth. What Lucifer was, he lost when he fell. He's the Lord of Hell, but as an angel, he presently ranks with the Elohim, alongside guardians, messengers and escorts." Mel unfolded herself from her armchair and crossed to the sofa to hug Patrick. "In the angelic hierarchy, you outrank him."

"But not for long," Patrick responded. "And not in your heart." The pain in his eyes broke her heart.

"If Luce wants to rise to his former position, he'll leave me far behind, for he won't have time for an Earth-bound angel when he's trying to regulate the rest of the universe. I'm partially responsible for him losing his high rank and it's only fitting that I help him regain it." Mel's heart still ached, but not just for Patrick now. For Luce's loss, too.

Patrick snorted softly. "You really mean it, don't you? If that's what he wanted, you'd work selflessly to restore him to his former glory, because you love him that much. You don't see him or yourself very clearly, then. That angel on the couch will never leave you. Pride and rank and position? He couldn't care less, as long as it's high enough for you, because he adores you. Loves you. He'd risk his very soul for you because this world wouldn't be the same without you."

Mel shook her head fiercely, pulling away from him. "You can't know that. You can't. No one would choose a paltry personal relationship over the fate of a world. Luce never noticed me when he was an angel before and he'll rise above me again, just you wait." She wiped away tears, hoping he didn't notice.

"No, the only angel who's that selfless is you. The rest of us aren't that perfect. Our personal relationships – those we love – are so important to us that they matter more to us than the fate of one world…or even the whole universe. I know that angel in there radiates so much love for you that his soul glows with it. And I know exactly what it feels like, so I know there's no way in Hell he'd let anything stand in his way of happiness with you, now that he's found you. Why have a lonely, loveless life with nothing but power when he could have you?" Patrick grinned. "Not even the devil's that stupid."

Thirty-four

Mel's phone vibrated in her pocket and she pulled it out. She answered the call on speaker so Patrick could hear, too. "Good morning, Koyane," she said.

"What time is it there? I waited as long as I could, as I didn't want to wake you up in case you wanted to sleep in on a Sunday morning."

Mel glanced at her watch. "It's just after three in the morning, but you didn't wake me. Patrick and I were still up."

"Three? Patrick? Are you in Ireland, then?

Does that mean you're busy with a crisis there?" Koyane's voice sounded strained.

"No, Patrick, Luce and I have been searching for Persephone. She's not here, so we spent a pleasant evening in the pub here in London." Mel counted the seconds in her head. Koyane was very much immersed in the Japanese culture of his home and he was meticulous about observing all the necessary pleasantries before getting down to business.

"Persephone? She was here not long ago, asking for directions and accommodation. I can speak to a few people here to find out if she's still here. If you want her, I'll send her directly to you."

"That would be lovely," Mel ventured, wondering what had motivated his call, seeing as it wasn't Persi.

"Mel, I need your help here in Tokyo."

She was shocked by the desperation in his tone. "With what, Koyane? I'm sure Persi won't be much trouble."

"With…we're facing a nuclear war over the Liancourt Rocks. They're fighting over fish and it was acrimonious enough before North

Korea sent a consultant in to assist with negotiations." Koyane paused and Mel waited for him to continue. "They sent Han Dong-Suk."

Patrick looked puzzled and Mel's thoughts weren't any clearer. "Mr Han has always been very cooperative in the past. Why is he suddenly a problem?"

"Because he wants to nuke the islands out of existence," Koyane said.

Patrick swore, drowning out Mel's less vociferous language.

She wet her lips. "When do you need me?"

"Yesterday," Koyane admitted.

Mel sighed. Tonight's karaoke had turned into farewell drinks with Patrick. "I'll make arrangements tonight. We'll try to find a flight that leaves London tomorrow, or as early as we can. It goes without saying: please do whatever you can to delay nuclear war until we get there."

"We? What are your accommodation requirements, Mere-san? One room for you and one for your staff? How many will you be bringing?"

Mel swallowed. "One room, two futons. We'll share."

"As you wish, Mere-san. I look forward to seeing you again."

"And I, you, Koyane." Mel ended the call.

Patrick shook his head. "You should be resting, not averting a nuclear holocaust."

Mel smiled. "Well, if there's a nuclear holocaust, the only place that'll be left to rest is Heaven, and I prefer to take my sabbaticals here on Earth, so I'd better make sure nothing blows up. Luce can come with me to take care of me." She rose. "I'd better get my laptop and book the flights. I'll pack in the morning when I've had some sleep."

Patrick followed her out to the living room. He nodded at Luce. "Do you want my help carrying him to bed?"

Mel shook her head. "No, he should be fine where he is. If you could find me a spare blanket for him, though, that'd be nice. I'll deal with his hangover." She knelt beside him and placed one hand on his forehead and the other over his liver. Concentrating, she broke down the alcohol in his blood into harmless molecules. She leaned over to kiss Luce's lips, but he didn't wake. Smiling, she covered him with the blanket Patrick had brought and stood.

"If you want, I'll take his place tonight so you don't feel lonely," Patrick offered, avoiding her eyes.

Mel crossed to his side and kissed his cheek. "It's a sweet thought, Patrick, but no. Luce might wake in the middle of the night and come join me. There isn't room for three of us in that bed. Thank you for everything you've done for us. I only wish we could stay longer, under more pleasant circumstances."

Thirty-five

Luce squinted at the sunlight lancing through the round window over the stairs. He knew the hangover headache would be epic this morning – just as soon as he lifted his head – and it just wasn't worth it if he didn't wake up with a woman by his side. Where was Mel?

"Mel?" he croaked, then cleared his throat and tried again. "Mel?" Louder, but still raspy.

She stepped into view and knelt beside him. "Good morning, my love. How are you feeling?" Tingling fingers touched his head.

His heart swelled with love for his angel. "You're taking away my hangover? You're an angel, Mel."

She laughed. "Actually, I took care of that last night. Though if you've forgotten I'm an angel, I'm worried. You should go have a shower after how hot and sweaty you were last night. Your clothes are hanging on the back of the bathroom door. We'll eat breakfast on the way to the airport. Now, shower, please. I'll have your coffee ready when you get out."

Luce rolled off the sofa, wincing in anticipation of the brain-blasting headache he half expected, but it was only his bladder that felt like it was going to explode. He beat a hasty retreat to the bathroom.

He showered, shaved and slipped on the shirt he'd last worn on the day they flew into London and it hit him – had Mel said they were going to the airport? Who were they picking up? Persephone? He cracked open the door. "Mel?" he called. "Why are we going to the airport?"

She wheeled her suitcase past the door and stopped. "Because we're flying to Japan."

He racked his brain, but he couldn't remember any mention of a Japanese trip. What else had he agreed to last night? "Um, why?"

"I need to stop some islands from being blown off the map. And Persi's there."

The nephilim was blowing things up? Wonderful. "What do you need me for?"

Mel's wicked smile appeared. "Moral support."

"Does that mean sex on demand? And you'll be on top?"

"Not on your demand, my love. Please put some pants on. We need to go soon." Mel and the suitcase disappeared down the stairs.

"Is Patrick coming with us?" he called after her.

"No, we're taking the Tube to Heathrow, then flying out at lunchtime. He's staying here."

Just the two of them? Luce could handle that. He couldn't wait to introduce Mel to the pleasures Japan had to offer. Not to mention the whisky.

Thirty-Six

"Please take the utmost care of her. See if you can persuade her to rest in Heaven instead. I've never seen her as exhausted as she was this trip. Please." Patrick's words echoed in Luce's head, accompanied by the memory of the saint's desperation as he'd shaken Luce's hand in farewell.

If Patrick was so worried for her, shouldn't he be, too? The shadows beneath Mel's eyes betrayed her lack of sleep and her reactions seemed slower than usual, too. Not so anyone else would notice – but he did.

"Your boarding pass, sir," the air hostess said, holding out the slip.

Luce peered at the seat allocation. "Which one's the window seat and which one's the aisle?"

The hostess inclined her head to read the printed text. "Neither, sir. These are in the middle of the centre row."

Luce threw it down on the counter. "You mean we're in the middle of the centre row in economy class for an overnight flight? No. Not a hope in Hell. We fly business or first class or not at all."

"Luce, it's fine. I had to book at the last minute so there's not much left in terms of seating choice, that's all. It's only twelve hours – it'll be fine," Mel said softly, gathering up the offending boarding passes.

"No, it isn't. I'll be carrying you off the plane in Tokyo if we take these tickets." Luce turned to the hostess. "We need two seats in business class. Together. And she gets the window seat."

She looked frightened. "But business class

costs more. You've only paid for economy…"

Luce yanked his platinum credit card out of his wallet. "Fix it, then."

"F-f-first class or business, sir?"

"Don't care as long as the two seats are together."

"Luce, I really don't need –" Mel began.

"You do. You absolutely do. I'm here to take care of you and that means a decent seat on the plane. A bed, even. The HELL Corporation can afford it. Are there two seats in first class?" Luce raised his eyebrows at the hostess.

"Yes, sir, but…" Fear seemed to have stolen her voice.

"Is there anything? Don't mind him. We were out late last night and neither of us has slept much as we didn't know we'd be flying today. I booked the tickets in the early hours of this morning and I'll be fine sitting wherever there's a seat on the plane. It's just urgent that we get there and I didn't really pay much attention to seats when I booked last night." Mel's sheepish smile seemed to set the girl at ease.

"Yes, ma'am, there are. In fact, there are only two first-class passengers on this flight. That means free upgrades are available and if no one else has upgraded yet..." She squinted at her screen, tapping at the keyboard with her manicured nails. "No, none yet. That means I can upgrade you for free." She smiled shyly. "I hope you reach Tokyo in time." She printed the new boarding passes and placed Luce's credit card on top. "Enjoy your flight."

Luce tucked his wallet back into his pocket as he hurried after Mel. "How did you do that?"

"I just read people well, Luce. She was thinking about how she fell asleep at her grandfather's funeral because she took the cheapest airfares and couldn't sleep on the long flight the night before. She assumed we were going for a funeral or something equally heartbreaking. Right now, she's hoping we make it in time and that her first-class upgrade will help us and somehow make up for what she missed." Mel joined the long queue at the security gates.

"Ah, Mel, we don't line up with everyone

else. First-class and business lounge customers are that way." Luce pointed at the near non-existent line beside the sign he'd just read aloud for her.

Mel shook her head as if to clear it. "Right. Sorry. I forgot." She dragged her feet after Luce.

He waited, then slipped an arm around her waist and pulled her to his side. Her exhaustion made her feel like she was sliding down to slump to the floor. Not if he could help it. "You're more tired than I am. You're just hiding it better. You should be flying home to rest, not heading into what sounds like a world of trouble. Mel, I need to know what's going on if I'm supposed to take care of you."

She lifted teary eyes to meet his gaze. "I can't ignore this, Luce, and I can't leave it to someone else. I don't know why it's come to this, either. When we reach Tokyo, believe me, I'll be looking for answers as much as you are. And if you could help me..." She exhaled slowly so that it sounded like a sigh. "That would be wonderful, Luce."

He laughed as he stepped through the body scanner. "It's only fair. I guess that makes me your personal assistant on this trip?"

Mel slipped her arm through his. "Very personal. I hope you don't mind sharing a room."

"Only if I get to sleep with you." He waited for her gentle remonstrance – he was definitely starting to like the way she said his name when she was embarrassed – but it never came. Too tired, he realised, pulling her close. He needed to take better care of her than ever.

Thirty-Seven

Mel's step seemed lighter as she led the way through the blocky buildings and forbidding concrete walls. The dreary grey was occasionally broken by a frothy pink tree that looked completely out of place among the gloomy houses. None of them looked like the sort of place Mel should be staying. The Tokyo hotels he'd stayed at in the past were all high-rises, the likes of which he didn't see here. If she'd paid little attention to their flight arrangements, did that mean she'd booked accommodation in a rat-infested warehouse?

"Mel?" She stopped and turned to smile, so Luce continued, "Which hotel did you say we were staying at?"

She laughed merrily. "Oh, no, we're not staying in a hotel. The rooms are tiny. No, we're staying in my friend's house." She pointed at a grey, two-storey building that looked no different to any of the others. "That one." She almost skipped across the street as Luce trundled along behind her with the suitcases.

Mel waited for him to catch up before she rang the bell. An intercom crackled to life with a man's voice speaking in what Luce presumed was Japanese. He didn't understand Mel's answer, either, but he was relieved when the door swung open.

Mel stepped inside and gestured for him to do the same. He came to an abrupt halt when he realised the concrete floor ended in a hefty step covered in slippers. The Japanese man standing at the top wore a plain leather pair, but the ones beside him could have been mistaken for fluffy rodents.

"Take your shoes off, my love, then choose some slippers," Mel whispered, slipping her feet into what Luce swore looked like a pair of eviscerated guinea pigs.

Gingerly, he kicked off his shoes and scanned the selection for something suitable. They all looked so small. Finally, he spotted some that looked like they might be big enough, hidden under a pair made of flaming red silk. Feeling completely ridiculous, he followed Mel's gaze to the man he presumed was her friend and their host.

"Koyane-san, thank you for your hospitality. May I present Luce Iblis, the CEO of the HELL Corporation, who will be assisting me." She turned to Luce. "This is Koyane of the Hashmallim. He's been guarding the leaders of this place since…ooh, how many millennia has it been, Koyane?"

"Not as long as you, Murielle-sama, which shows in our present difficulties," Koyane replied with a bow. "Please, permit me to make you some tea?"

Mel agreed, and she and Luce followed Koyane to a room with a low, square table but no chairs.

"Please," Koyane said, gesturing at the table before he departed through a screen door.

"Um, Mel? What are we supposed to do?"

She stared at him. "I thought you'd been to Japan. I'm sure I remember you telling me about how you introduced Persi to Japanese whisky."

Luce didn't think he could feel more uncomfortable, but if anything, it was getting worse. "I stayed in a hotel and we ate at restaurants all the time. No houses or supermarkets or things that normal people who live here do. I was here on business, not on holiday."

"Were your business dealings successful?" Mel's eyes seemed to see into his soul. Hell, he knew they could.

"No. We didn't manage to secure a single contract in Japan," he admitted.

She smiled. "I might be able to help you with that, as long as you make it your business to learn about Japanese culture while we're here. Take the table." She waved at it. "We're supposed to kneel on the mats around it.

Cushions are –" She slid open a cupboard and tossed a stack to Luce "– here. Koyane will bring tea and we'll talk."

Almost as if he'd been summoned by her words, Koyane slid the screen open and carried a tray filled with all the accoutrements for tea, without the traditional ceremony.

Mel's eyes widened in delight. "Ohh, sakura manju! I've missed those. This is bribery of the best kind. You're sweetening me up for bad news, aren't you?"

For the first time, Koyane smiled. "Mere-san, no one's sweeter than you."

An angel in every port. Koyane was Mel's Tokyo Patrick, Luce realised with dread. First nuclear war; now he'd have to fight for Mel's attention here, too. Hell, could it get any worse?

Thirty-eight

"How was London, Mere-san?" Koyane asked as he poured the tea.

"Fun, but also a waste of time," Mel said, looking longingly at the cakes. "We knew Persi had gone to Ireland, but the trail came to a dead end. Patrick tracked her to one of his favourite haunts and then she disappeared. But I did learn something useful – I discovered that Luce here is quite the karaoke king." She beamed at Luce.

"He's not a king, he's a dick. He's all show

and seduction with no substance. He's not even all that good-looking. And he's wearing my brother's slippers."

Three pairs of eyes zeroed in on the doorway and a pouting Japanese girl dressed entirely in red to match her flaming hair.

"He tried to sell his shoddy company's services to the Japanese government so he could replace thousands of salaried Japanese people with his own imported workers. Now, no one in Japan's buying what he's selling." She sashayed into the room and knelt smoothly. "But this must be the beautiful Murielle-sama I've heard paeans of praise about. They fell woefully short of reality. I am honoured to finally meet you, Murielle-sama." She bowed so low, her forehead almost touched the mat.

Koyane coughed uncomfortably. "Ah, Keiko, this is Murielle-sama, and I believe you already know Luce Iblis? Keiko is caught up in this island business, too, so I asked her to join us. This is Keiko Taniwha."

Luce wasn't sure which of them hated the other more — the girl's vitriol made it clear she couldn't stand him, and he was rapidly making plans for her place in Hell after she was dead. Sooner rather than later, if he had any say in it.

"One of the Pacific people – the first I have met. The honour is mine, Keiko-san," Mel said, bowing. "I think you will find that Luce has changed much since you last met him. He is here at my invitation, because I desire his assistance."

Keiko burst into high-pitched giggles, reminding Luce painfully of Persephone. It seemed to have the same effect on Koyane, too.

"I was just about to tell Mere-san about her cousin Persephone's visit, so your timing is perfect, Keiko," Koyane said, sipping his tea. He set the cup down with a tiny clink. "Persephone arrived here just over a week ago. She came straight to me, asking for assistance in finding accommodation near Beppu as she was fascinated by the jigoku near there. She said she was investigating something for you, Mere-san, so I sent her to Homusubi, one of the present Dynameis in our region. He knows more about the jigoku than I ever will."

Luce raised his hand. "Can I have an interpreter, please? Not all of us speak Japanese."

Mel held up her hand in response. "How about me? Beppu is a city on the island of Kyushu to the south of here. Homusubi is one of the Dynameis. His speciality is volcanoes and vents and he's particularly proud of the jigoku, which roughly translates to hells. The jigoku are volcanic hot springs near Beppu. The colours are really quite beautiful, or so I have heard." She smiled. "Does that cover it, my love?"

Keiko snorted and started tapping her teeth with one ruby-tinted fingernail.

Luce nodded.

"Just let me know if you need the background on anything else," she whispered, then raised her voice again. "So she's in Beppu?"

"I don't know," Koyane admitted. "Since she left, I've heard nothing from her. I mentioned it to Keiko yesterday and she offered to make some enquiries. Can you offer Mere-san anything further, Keiko?"

Keiko shrugged. "Nothing. No one seems to have seen her since the day she arrived. Your friend Homusubi met her and answered a number of questions, but she never returned." She laughed. "Good riddance, I say. That girl is trouble. I'm surprised you'd trust her out on her own, Murielle-sama. She couldn't get a coffee from a vending machine, much less find any information of value to you. Maybe the kappa got her."

"Uh, kappa?" Luce interjected.

This time Keiko grinned. "A kappa is a scaly, colour-changing monster of myth that lives underwater in the region around Beppu. They like to prey on women. Actually, the kappa at Beppu is my grandfather on my mother's side, so I spoke to him, too. He said she was too skinny and whiny for his taste. And he prefers girls who wear underwear."

Luce laughed so hard he nearly choked. Maybe Keiko wasn't so bad, after all. Her perceptions of Persephone were pretty close to his own. But if she was the granddaughter of a monster, what did that make her? An underwater creature that preyed on men?

Mel caught his eye and nodded silently.

Damn. Maybe Keiko wasn't going to Hell, either. Pity. She'd have made a good harpy.

"So Persi was here in Japan a week ago, but now she's gone? Oh well, thank you. At least we're one step closer to finding her, even if I have no idea what she was doing here. I certainly didn't send her, so whatever mission she's on is one of her own making." Mel lifted her cup in both hands and inhaled deeply before sipping at the contents. Her happy smile told Luce he needed to drink some, too.

The tea was so bitter that Luce choked on his first mouthful. How could Mel tolerate the horrible stuff?

Still smiling, she sank her teeth into one of the pink, round cakes, revealing a darker pink interior. Mel offered the cake to Luce. "Take a bite of this; then, with the sweetness still on your tongue, taste the tea."

Luce hesitated. Koyane seemed intent on his own tea, but Keiko was watching him as if she was just waiting for him to make a fool out of himself. Mel wouldn't give him bad advice, would she?

"They're my favourite, so if you don't take it, I'll happily eat the whole thing myself. Maybe even the whole plate," Mel said. Her eyes danced with restrained laughter.

Luce leaned forward and nibbled on the edge of the cake. It tasted of sugar with a faint hint of flowers and fruit, so he took a bigger bite. With his mouth full of the sticky stuff – what had Mel called it? Oh, that's right, a manju – Luce slurped his tea. His eyes widened in surprise. Of course, Mel was right.

"I could live on these," Mel said, then laughed. "Well, if I could live on cake and tea." She straightened and her smile faded. "Okay, you've well and truly sweetened me up. Time to hit me with the bad news, Koyane."

Thirty–nine

Glances darted between Koyane and Keiko until Luce wanted to smash their heads together. "Just spit it out," Luce snapped. "We didn't fly halfway around the world to watch you two make goo-goo eyes at each other."

Koyane sighed. "The difficulty lies in Keiko's secrets, which are not mine to tell."

Mel gave a tiny smile. "Would it be enough to say that she, like the rest of us, isn't human, and leave it at that?"

Keiko nodded gratefully. "The problem is

the Liancourt Rocks. People here call them Takeshima and Koreans call them Dokdo, but neither can agree on who owns them. They're rocks in the middle of the East Sea – the people here call it the Sea of Japan. So many names, it's hard to keep track. And that's what makes it worse. Both countries claim them and they were brilliant for fishing. But with both countries fishing around them, that's no longer the case. Some species haven't been seen there for over fifty years – it's not just overfishing, it's extinction."

Who'd have guessed? The girl was an environmentalist at heart. Or was the little sea monster just protecting her own food supply?

"To force a solution, my people decided the best way to do this was to propose a business arrangement that benefited both countries."

There was a whole society of sea monsters? Luce tried not to grin. He wondered if the men found prickly Keiko attractive.

"The proposal is an abalone farm, where the shellfish is processed on-site into a superior dried product, though we'll be using traditional recipes." Keiko grinned. "My grandmother's secret recipe, in fact.

"Now, in order to protect our stocks and sea cages, we require assurances that no Japanese, Korean or foreign fishing activities occur within our little fish farm, and either the authority to police it, or assistance from both countries. The price we pay for this will be in the form of concessions to both Japan and Korea in pricing our product. We sell it to them cheaply, up to a particular quota. I have investors from both countries backing this project, so it's an international company, neither Korean nor Japanese."

"How do they feel about a Japanese girl in charge, or were you thinking of letting someone else manage your farm?" Luce asked. Being the devil had its high points – you never played the devil's advocate when you worked on your own behalf. It was cheaper, too.

Keiko shot him a withering glance. "I am a citizen of New Zealand, where I was born." She cleared her throat and continued, "Everything was going swimmingly, with both Japanese and South Korean authorities willing to come to some sort of terms. Until they set a date for formal discussions to take place and decided that they needed a North Korean delegate present. North Korea engaged a consultant to represent them – Han Dong-Suk."

Luce burst out laughing. "You're kidding me, right? That can't be a real name!"

"Mr Han is a businessman whose main business interests involve the facility management of nuclear power plants," Mel said softly. "He most certainly is real, and even more real is the lesser-known fact that he has access to North Korea's nuclear arsenal because of his experience with radiation containment. And with his political contacts in North Korea, he's usually a stabilising element, not a disruptive one." Mel turned shrewd eyes on Koyane and Keiko. "What's changed for Mr Han?"

Keiko giggled. "He acquired a new asset. Her name is Sun-Hee and she's quite the little socialite. And now Mr Han is hell-bent on destroying my islands as a token of his love for his bride."

Nothing expressed his power and virility

like vaporising entire islands with a nuclear arsenal, Luce guessed. Humans could be so stupid sometimes. He bet the man couldn't satisfy his wife – that'd be why he felt the need to nuke things instead.

"Why?" Mel asked.

Luce opened his mouth to tell her his idea, then closed it to glare at Keiko, who was still giggling.

"Apparently it's a doomed wartime romance," Keiko cooed. "Sun-Hee's grandmother or great-grandmother was in love with a man who came home safe from the Second World War, only to take up fishing. Because that was much safer. The Americans used the Rocks as a bombing range after the war, but the Korean fishermen didn't know that, so they were out fishing in the waters around the Rocks when some US planes flew in from the east and bombs rained from the sky. The woman's sweetheart was one of the unlucky ones – his boat got hit and he didn't come home. Sun-Hee was named for the old lady, who told her the tale when she was a little girl. To hear the grandmother tell it, those islands are a blight on the world. If they hadn't existed, then she wouldn't have lost the love of her life and been forced to marry her worthless husband, Sun-Hee's grandfather. Great-grandfather? Whatever. She told the story to Han once and he swore to level the islands to the ground before he lets anyone else bomb them."

"Vaporising them before someone else can? That makes sense," Luce joked.

"No it doesn't, stupid. Or not to anyone who isn't thinking with his dick, anyway." Keiko eyed his pants with a disdainful sniff. "Destroying the islands above the waterline will kill fish locally and pollute water and air for miles around, making the present situation even worse. At least with the islands there, contested between two countries, no one else is going to bomb them."

Luce opened his mouth to respond, but Mel's calming hand over his distracted him.

"I believe Luce was joking, Keiko-san," she said. "I'm sure he understands the gravity of the situation as clearly as any of us. You're planning a business venture at these islands and you'd like it to succeed for both personal and professional reasons; the Korean and Japanese governments, despite a long history of disagreement over the islands' ownership, are willing to reach some sort of compromise because they support what could be a highly lucrative business; yet Mr Han has brought all this cooperation to a standstill by his desire to please his wife by making a statement of power and military might." She scanned their faces. "So, it's simple. The key is Mrs Han. We need to get her to call off her husband."

"We've tried that," Keiko said glumly. "She's told him many times she doesn't care about the islands and she wouldn't notice if he giftwrapped them or bombed them out of existence. And her husband won't budge." She stared intently at Mel. "Murielle-san, I've heard that you're a miracle worker. We'll need one of your miracles now. I've secured invitations to a private party the Hans are holding so you can meet them tonight."

Mel beamed. "A party sounds lovely. Luce, you did bring a suit, didn't you?"

Forty

"Let me take a picture," Luce begged, holding up his phone. He'd never used its camera before, but how hard could it be?

"Of what?"

"How lovely you look tonight," he replied, tapping the button which he hoped would take a picture. "You know I love you, right?"

She laughed and blushed. "And I love you, Luce."

Mel looked absolutely beautiful. Her cocktail dress was gold silk that shimmered and her only jewellery was a string of creamy-gold pearls that he'd never seen before.

"Where did you get those?" he whispered, caressing her neck. They were definitely real, but such an unusual colour.

She ducked her head. "They were a gift from a friend, a long time ago. Every time I've tried to part with them, they always seem to return to me, so I've decided to keep them. They feel almost like old friends themselves, after all this time."

Luce mentally kicked himself for not having bought her jewellery. He'd never seen her wear any before, but now that he had, he could correct his mistake. Hopefully. "A friend? Or a lover? Was it Patrick? Or Koyane?"

Mel laughed softly. "No, none of them. They were a gift from a grateful human leader."

They moved up in the receiving line until they faced their hosts.

"Han-san, may I present Murielle-san, who you already know, and Mr Luce Iblis, the CEO of the HELL Corporation?" Keiko said.

Han inclined his head in a disinterested bow

and turned his attention to the people behind them. At his side, the Korean girl dressed in something pink and frilly stared avidly at them, wiggling as if she was trying to dislodge a spider that had slipped inside the pink dress. Keiko repeated her introduction to Sun-Hee, who erupted in a fountain of giggles that grated on Luce's ear. It didn't help that this girl could have passed for Persephone's sister.

"Call me Sunny, Mr Iblis," she simpered, stretching up to kiss his cheeks. She dropped her voice to a whisper. "My friend Keiko says you're a dick. I'd like to see that." She reached down and squeezed.

Luce pried her fingers loose and stepped back. "Mrs Han, that will land you in a world of trouble that you can't handle."

This only seemed to excite her further. "Oh, I love trouble, Mr Iblis. In fact, I'm often a very bad girl."

Though he tried to resist it, the image of Level Two in Hell popped into his head and wouldn't leave. "Be careful, then. I know the punishment for bad girls."

"I bet you do," she breathed. "I'd love you

to show me some time." She gave him a smouldering look until Luce wanted to upend a jug of cold water over her head. Stupid human had no idea.

Sunny had only a bored bow for Mel before turning her attention to the next guest.

Mel took Luce's arm and walked him over to a waiter, who offered them drinks. Mel sipped her ice wine until the waiter moved out of earshot, when she whispered, "Looks like Sun-Hee took quite a shine to you. I'm sure with all your wit and charm, you'll have no problem persuading her to speak to her husband on our behalf. When we get home, I'll be able to tell everyone that you're the angel who averted nuclear war."

His perfect angel in gold silk or her irritating cousin's doppelganger – what a choice! As he stared at her longingly, Mel winked. "Just as long as you come home with me tonight. I admit I've been thinking about sharing a futon with you since I first booked the flights." She reached for a waiter's tray and snagged another glass of wine. "Here, go take her a drink. She looks lonely and bored. Just make sure she enjoys her night."

"What about you?" He wasn't sacrificing Mel's night for some woman he didn't know.

Mel smiled. "I'm working, too. I figured you'd be spending the evening with Mr Han, businessman to businessman, but if you're taking care of his wife, then I'll have to do my best to take your place. The sooner we get this situation sorted, the sooner we can go home."

It sounded so simple. And Mel was never wrong, right?

Luce winked and headed for the listless-looking Sunny, who lit right up the moment she saw him. "You look like you need a drink," he said, offering her a wineglass.

She snatched the glass from his hand and beamed back. "Ah-ah-ah, Mr Iblis, I think you're trying to get me drunk so I'll tell you my husband's secrets."

Luce grinned. "Actually, I was hoping you'd spill some of yours."

Her shock was faked, he was sure of it. "Mr Iblis! I'm sure I have no secrets." She smiled coyly. "Oh, maybe just one or two."

He stood beside her, sipping his drink,

waiting for her to continue. He had no idea how to make small talk with a woman like this. He was much more comfortable ordering them around.

"You're not like my husband or any of his boring businessman friends. I bet you're not like them in bed, either. I bet you know exactly what you want and just how to get it." She punctuated the last few words by poking him in the chest.

He brushed her hand away. "Mrs Han, no man's as good as me in bed, on the desk or occasionally even up against the bookcase in my office. And if you touch me without my permission one more time, I might just have to get the handcuffs out."

Her excited gasp told him he'd guessed right. "Mr Iblis! Why, I'm shocked. I'll tell you what. I'll trade you a secret for one of yours."

Luce shrugged. "Sure. You first. Why would a happily married woman flirt so outrageously with a businessman she barely knows?"

She smacked his arm lightly. "What a naughty question! I'll tell you, but not here. How about in the library?"

Library? This woman didn't seem like much of a reader. Not like Mel. She devoured books on her phone like he couldn't believe. He followed Sunny out of the reception room and through three sets of sliding screens before they reached a timber-floored passage. The passage ended in another screen, which slid sibilantly aside to reveal walls lined with bookcases. A desk stood in the middle, pushed up against a pink chaise longue that looked exactly the right size for the diminutive woman in front of him.

She spun on the spot, waving her hands at the shelves. "This is where I keep my CEOs, billionaires, Navy SEALs, rock stars, bikers...ooh, and MMA fighters. Every one of them strong and masterful, powerful enough to bend any woman to their will."

Luce looked more closely at the shelves. If he didn't know better, he might be in the harpies' private library on Level Seven. The books were all tattered paperbacks full of men the likes of which he'd never met. "Fictional heroes. Men who don't exist outside of books," he dismissed them.

"You're here. And you're not in a book," she teased.

"Are you going to answer the question I asked earlier? Now we're here in private and all?"

Her little pink tongue darted out and wet her lips. Between that and the playful look in her eyes, she reminded him of a kitten. A tiny, cute-looking bundle until it sank all its needle-sharp teeth and claws into you for daring to touch it. Luce hated kittens almost as much as he'd been scared of swans.

"My marriage is one of convenience. I made him wait until after marriage for sex, because I believed it was the correct thing to do, but it appears he only agreed to it because he never wanted me in the first place. I stand at his side in functions like this one, but it's a sham, Mr Iblis. I married a man I thought would have the power to take me as hard as any of these book heroes, but he never has. Not even on our wedding night – he never came to my bed." She grabbed the hem of her black dress and jerked it up to her waist, revealing black stockings and bare skin, before bending over the desk. "You're man enough, aren't you, Mr Iblis? Take me. Take me now."

She could have been Persephone's sister for sure. What was wrong with her? And what would Mel think if she saw this?

"Mrs Han, I can't. I have –"

"Ten seconds to bury yourself balls deep in my cunt or I'll call security and tell them you forced me. Japan has strict penalties for rapists."

Mel would kill him. No matter what he did, she'd kill him. So which was the lesser of two evils? Taking his pleasure of this willing woman and turning her into an adulterer, or getting arrested and ruining Mel's evening, as well as any chance they had at getting on this crazy woman's good side?

"What about foreplay?" Luce asked weakly.

She yanked open a drawer beside her leg, revealing an impressive array of vibrators and other toys. "As long as you fuck me, you can do anything you want. Do I have to beg, Mr Iblis?"

Ugh, no. Mel had told him to make sure this woman enjoyed her night. Charm her, she'd said. This woman didn't want charm. She wanted to be fucked roughly like some nameless PA on his desk, like he'd done when he was a demon.

"Please, Mr Iblis," she simpered, giving him a look that she probably thought was sweet.

Swallowing, Luce strode forward and placed his hand at the back of her neck. "Keep your head down. No eye contact until I say so. Hold on to the edge of the desk with both hands. Brace yourself. I'm going to fuck you so hard, you'll be feeling my cock all week." Imagining it, more like, he thought as he picked up a dildo from the drawer.

Forty-one

"Murielle-san, it's been a long time."

Mel turned with an automatic smile for the man behind her. "Director, I'm sure it's only been two years since the tsunami."

Han Dong-Suk frowned, filling his plate with items from the buffet. "The tsunami? I forgot you were there. I was so busy handling press about that nuclear power plant that got hit…and then having to upgrade all the facilities on the mainland. It's been a very busy few years. But good ones, for that's how I met my wife, Sun-Hee. She was at a fundraiser to assist those left homeless by the tsunami. I am afraid I've had eyes for no other woman since." He smiled, but still seemed sad.

"I heard that you'd finally discovered love. Congratulations, Director. I'm very happy for you. I sincerely hope you'll both be very happy together." She couldn't say that she knew, for the future of this couple was clouded. Perhaps by her own interference, she thought uneasily.

He sighed heavily. "So do I, but Sun-Hee is not the girl I fell in love with. She's changed, grown cold. And I have no idea what I've done."

Mel was surprised by his confession for he barely knew her, but perhaps his desperation had made him forget that. The man definitely did look desperate. "What do you mean, cold?"

Mr Han hesitated before exclaiming, "You're a woman, Murielle-san. You understand love. Perhaps you can explain to me why a woman who spent months kissing and flirting with me, building anticipation that on our wedding night she would be mine – it is no exaggeration, for she said those words, many times – would completely avoid my bed once we were married?"

Advising a man on marital relations with his wife? Mel blushed deeply. She wished Luce were with her. He'd know what to say. Possibly even offer a few tips from his extensive experience. Where was Luce? She glanced around, but didn't see him. She didn't see Mrs Han, either, so she figured he must be off taking care of her.

She coughed discreetly. "Director, do you think perhaps it was because she was surprised by her first relations with you on your wedding night?" She didn't dare say that his performance might have been lacking, though she knew it was the most likely source of his wife's dissatisfaction.

He laughed harshly. "What relations? She gave me a kiss full of promise and said she would change clothes. I retired to my room, specially prepared for us with all sorts of strange things – rose petals and candles and all manner of romantic ideas – but she never came. I thought of going to her room to ask what kept her so long, but a lady likes to take her time and my Sun-Hee is no exception, so I waited. When morning came, I had those infernal petals stuck to my body instead of my lovely wife. She never came." His voice wavered as if he might cry.

Mel tried to hide her shock. "What did you say when you saw her the next morning?"

He reddened. "I was furious. I wanted to demand to know why she would tease me and yet do nothing, but I was summoned to work before she awoke. When I saw her that evening, she avoided even looking at me and I knew I couldn't be angry at her, as I must have done something wrong."

"Have you tried just asking her?"

He guffawed. "Me, a crusty old businessman, ask my young flower of a wife for sex? Never. I am too proud to beg, even of the woman I love. And I will not force myself on her by demanding her submission – that sort of thing is for barbarians. She once joked that she was marrying the most powerful man in Korea, but she holds my heart in her fist and I am powerless against her. Do you think I am just a silly old man, Murielle-san?"

He was only ten years older than his bride – and hardly an old man, though not a young one, either. Mel shook her head emphatically and said, "No, Director. Love makes fools of us all. Have you not asked her?"

"I tried to ask her once whether she regretted marrying me. She grew angry and told me she would not regret it if I proved that I was the powerful man she thought I was. So I looked for a way to show this power that would demonstrate to my disappointed wife that I am worthy of her. What could no other man do? Why, I could level the islands where her illustrious ancestress and namesake lost her love, as a fitting memorial to the man who should have been her ancestor." His eyes blazed as if reflecting the flash from the atomic blast in his imagination.

Mel shivered. She'd seen what those blasts did to people – no, more than seen it. She'd felt the agony of flesh searing through her bones as her shadow burned into stone in Hiroshima, then again in Nagasaki. Then rebuilt her body a third time to seek Japan's surrender on behalf of those who'd died screaming with her. She'd seen suffering the likes of which no one else had, for the souls of those who died had continued to broadcast their pain even after death. And she'd stayed to coordinate the army of escort angels who had come to claim their souls.

"Director, have you ever visited the Hiroshima Peace Memorial? I find the pictures there quite haunting – the effects of an atomic blast are horrifying. It shows what too much power can do when it's used as a weapon."

He grunted. "I don't have time to play tourist when I'm in Japan. Not when I'm here on business."

"I'd call it professional interest, if nothing else. If you intend to level the islands of Dokdo, I recommend that you find out more about the power you wield."

His eyes narrowed. "So, it's true. You are here for the negotiations. May I ask whose side you're on when it comes to Dokdo? Whoever has engaged your valuable services usually emerges victorious, I've found." His tone made it sound like a joke, but his eyes were deadly serious. Han Dong-Suk was a shrewd businessman who knew which way the wind was blowing – and if he didn't, he certainly wanted to.

Mel ducked her head. "I'm just an adviser, Director. My clients pay for my advice, but it doesn't mean they have to follow it. The mediator on this matter is my friend, Koyane, who brought me in to assist. My client is Keiko Taniwha – the proponent whose proposal invoked this furore. Like Koyane and Keiko, I seek only a swift resolution."

"So do I, Murielle-san. And I find actions speak louder than words. Please excuse me, I must see to my other guests." He bowed and hurried away.

Mel sighed. When it came to a man's ego, his bedroom skills and his heart, he was as unreasonable as the next guy. She only hoped Luce was making better progress with the man's wife.

Forty-two

A tiny dog yapped in someone's garden, sounding almost identical to Sunny's joyful yelps when Luce had capitulated to her begging and plied the flogger. Luce cringed inwardly, wishing he could bleach the memory from his brain. He wasn't a demon any more and corrupting souls like that woman's wasn't something he did, let alone enjoyed. God, had he ever felt so cheap? He was an angel now – Mel had said so, and she was never wrong. He didn't need to be some lonely trophy wife's gigolo. What would Mel say if and when he told her? If she didn't know already from reading his mind. What must she think of him? He glanced at Mel, who gave him a tired smile. Her evening hadn't gone well, either, he deduced, though she hadn't said why or how.

As soon as they reached Koyane's house, Luce said, "Hell, I need a shower. Anyone mind if I take the first one?"

The silence lasted for a long moment before Koyane said, "Usually guests have first use of the bath in the evening, but as one of the guests is Murielle-sama…"

"I'll be really quick, Luce, and you can even join me if you want," Mel said.

Tempting as this was, Luce needed to scrub himself several times with plenty of soap before he dared touch her. That crazy Korean girl left him feeling soiled inside and out, even if he had kept his clothes on. He'd already washed his hands more than a dozen times, but they didn't feel clean enough. "Maybe. I just…really want a shower."

He followed Mel to the rice-paper-screened room they shared and dug out some clean clothes. He waited for her to lead the way to the bathroom.

"You put your clothes here," Mel said, placing hers neatly in a pile on the shelf. Luce bundled his up into a ball and laid them beside hers. "Then you strip off and take your toiletries through to the bathroom."

The sight of Mel's dress slipping down over her hips and sliding to the floor left him mesmerised. He couldn't take his eyes off her when her underwear followed.

"Come through when you're ready," Mel said over her shoulder as she padded through the door, which closed behind her.

Luce stripped, leaving his clothes in a pile on the floor. He didn't want to wear that suit ever again. That woman had touched it. He shuddered. He needed a hot shower and plenty of soap and disinfectant. Then, if he was really lucky, Mel's warm hands to drive the thoughts of any other woman out of his head.

He opened the door, unleashing a cloud of steam, and stepped inside. He was just in time to see Mel step into the boxy wooden bathtub. She turned her blissful smile on him. "First, you have a shower and wash yourself all over with soap, then rinse it off before taking a hot bath. Koyane swears by having a cedar tub and every time I sink into the hot water, I think I agree with him. You should see the ones at his house in Kyoto."

The shower didn't have a cubicle to separate it from the rest of the tiled room, so Luce just turned the hot tap on full and let the steaming water gush over him for a few minutes, wishing it could burn away the sensation of his skin crawling. He squeezed out half a bottle of shower gel, rubbing it briskly all over his body until he was covered in thick foam. Another deluge of hot water sluiced it off him before he repeated the whole process. And a third time, opening a fresh bottle of soap. He was reaching down to scrub the stuff down his legs when soft, wet skin bumped him from behind.

"My love, may I join you? I'll wash your back, if you like." Cool liquid oozed onto his back, followed by the light touch of Mel's warm hands.

Heaven. A shower with his angel would be Heaven. "Please," he breathed. Luce closed his eyes and stood still as Mel's fingers worked her healing magic on him. A sublime angel who shouldn't soil herself by touching a damaged devil. An angel who deserved to know what he'd done. Luce forced himself to say, "Mel, please forgive me. I –"

"There's nothing to forgive."

He swore he could hear her smiling. Luce glanced over his soapy shoulder. Her eyes were alight with so much love he couldn't bear to look away. Or admit how he'd betrayed her.

"I love you," he said instead. "I love you more than anyone or anything else, ever. When this world ends, no, when this entire universe ends, I'll still love you, Melody."

"I love you, too, Luce. Time to wash off this soap, though. Turn around and I'll do your front."

Luce obediently rotated and was rewarded with a passionate kiss as Mel pressed her body against his. How could he want anyone else when he had Mel? Her touch burned away all the distasteful memories. He wanted…no, more than just want; his need for her was so powerful he'd explode if she pushed him away or even stopped kissing him. He could feel the love radiating from her, coursing through their kiss like a relentless river that dragged him deeper and deeper into where he longed to go.

What would she do when she found out what he'd done with that horrible Han woman? When she knew he'd reverted back to his old, demonic ways? Was his soul tainted now, too? He couldn't stand to lose Mel.

"Oh God, Melody. I love you so much." He wrapped his arms around her, holding her so tightly that all he could feel was her skin against his. "And I need you. Please, can we —"

"Yes. Ohh, yes. But not here. Keiko and Koyane are waiting to use the bath after us. We can and we will, in the privacy of our room. Don't take too long in the bath, or I might fall asleep waiting for you, and neither of us wants that." Her eyes were filled with love as she surveyed his body.

"To Hell with a bath. All I want is you." Luce wrenched the taps off and walked her to the door. The chilly air in the dressing room was a shock compared to the heady steam in the bathroom, but Luce gritted his teeth and quickly towelled himself dry so he could pull on enough clothes to pass as decent for the short walk back to their room.

He glanced at Mel to find her already wrapped in a cotton kimono patterned with pink flowers. She leaned over to gather up their dirty clothes and tossed them into the laundry hamper. "I'll deal with those tomorrow. But now…come with me?"

Luce grabbed her outstretched hand and together they burst through the dressing room door into the passage beyond, startling Keiko in her red kimono right outside, but they didn't stop. Mel called something over her shoulder in breathless Japanese that Luce didn't understand, but he didn't need a translation. He needed Mel.

He slid the screen door shut behind him and struggled to rid himself of his shorts, which clung to his still-damp legs as if they were trying to restrain him from reaching Mel. And Mel… "My God," he whispered reverently. Mel hadn't donned anything beneath her kimono and the pink-flowered cotton now hung from a wall hook.

The shorts finally yielded and Luce dropped to his knees on the futon laid out on the tatami floor.

Mel gave him a gentle smile. "Come to bed with me, my love."

Forty-three

Luce was woken by light filtering through the paper screens, but he didn't want to move. He held Mel securely in his arms. As long as she was still asleep, he wasn't letting go any time soon. Melody. Heaven. He closed his eyes and inhaled the scent of her hair. Myrrh and lemon, neroli and coconut…

"Good morning, my love." Mel tilted her head back to claim a kiss that Luce couldn't deny her. She shifted and the bliss of her skin sliding against his reminded him why they were still naked.

Though he wanted to give her his full attention, Luce's eyes kept darting to the door.

"What is it?"

"I expect Patrick to come bursting in," Luce admitted.

Mel laughed gently. "Patrick is still in London, unless he's headed back to Ireland or somewhere he's needed. We're here with Koyane and Keiko. Koyane would never invade a guest's privacy like that. But he will have breakfast and tea waiting for us in the kitchen."

"Coffee?" Luce asked hopefully.

"Probably. I suspect he'd have it for Keiko and maybe some of the others. Ohh, I hope he had time to get some Nagano apples. You wait. I bet you've never seen anything like them."

Nagano apples? Wasn't that the skiing place? How did you ski around apple trees? Luce figured he'd look stupid if he asked, so he dug through his luggage instead. "Are we in negotiations today or are we tourists?" he asked over his shoulder.

"Mm, not sure," Mel replied, her voice slightly muffled as she pulled something over her head. "Koyane will tell us, but I suspect we'll be in negotiations. That means sober suits so we blend in."

Luce laughed. "You? Blend in? With your glowing golden hair and your suit only slightly darker? You're a sunbeam at midnight, Melody – no one will be able to pay attention to anyone else." He drank her in and realised her appearance was changing. The glow was fading and even her hair looked darker. "Hey, what did you just do?"

She blushed. "With you, I'm myself. No fetters, no restraints. But today I'm Murielle D'Angelo, a political adviser with a well-earned reputation – one which Koyane intends to use to effect in international negotiations. But a political adviser requires the perception of darkness and not light, hence my light must be hidden."

Luce studied Mel as she buttoned her blazer. She was right, he decided – she could blend in like this. As if she'd heard the thought, Mel lifted her chin so her gaze met his. Ah, there it was – not all of her glow was gone. It smouldered behind her grey eyes, imbuing her with an otherworldly presence that was at once powerful, threatening and enticing. "Do I have to call you Murielle? I might forget and call you Mel."

Mel waved away his worries. "No, Mel's fine. It's not a nickname many others know here, so if you're talking about me, you might want to use Murielle, that's all." She waited for him to finish buckling his belt. "You'll probably need a tie with that today, and the jacket."

Luce nodded and slipped an arm around her waist. "Let's go find breakfast first. And I'll pray for a coffee."

Mel led the way to the kitchen.

"*Ohayo gozaimasu*, Mere-san," Koyane greeted her, bowing.

"*Ohayo*, Koyane," Mel replied, nodding her thanks as he poured her a cup of tea.

Lucifer gritted his teeth. He hoped he didn't have to respond to whatever the Japanese man had said.

"Good morning, Lucifer. I hope everything

in your room meets your expectations. If you need anything, please do not hesitate to ask." Koyane's head-bob was nowhere near as respectful as the bow he'd offered Mel, but that was fair enough.

"Everything's fine. Mel's been explaining things to me – the shower, the bath, the beds on the floor, everything. What I need now is coffee," Luce replied, feeling an unfamiliar rush of gratitude toward the man.

"Mere-san is often very busy, so if she is not available, you may ask me anything," Koyane said gravely. He broke into a smile. "I have heard of your taste for coffee. I hope my machine will answer to your needs." He waved at a brand-new coffee machine on the bench.

Luce whistled and glanced at Mel, who shook her head. Where had the Japanese man heard stories from? Luce groaned. "Tell me you haven't heard crazy stories from Persephone."

"Patrick called me while you were flying. He said that I should make sure I could provide good coffee, or my guest might cause a stir as he runs down the street naked to purchase one." Koyane laughed and leaned forward. "Tell me: did you really do it?"

Luce shifted uncomfortably. "No. Patrick warned me that I'd need to put pants on or I'd get arrested."

To cover Luce's embarrassment, Mel changed the subject. "Where's Keiko? Is she still asleep?"

Koyane coughed. "Ah, no. She prefers her breakfast fresh, so she eats at the Tsukiji markets. She should be home soon."

Mel hid a smile behind her teacup and Luce wondered what the joke was.

Speak of the devil.

Keiko breezed in, carrying a faint whiff of fish and a bag full of paper-wrapped packages. "I brought breakfast!" she announced, setting her bag on the counter.

Luce kept his distance, particularly when the smell of fish intensified.

"Fresh this morning!" The thin-sliced raw fish certainly looked fresh, but the thought of eating it for breakfast made Luce's stomach churn. "And pastries for you, Murielle-sama." Another box revealed an impressive selection of French confections.

Luce hid his grin when Mel picked out an almond croissant, then offered the box to him. "There's another one in here, my love. Japanese patisseries are nothing short of amazing."

As they ate, Koyane explained that the negotiations were scheduled for over the next three days, so it was a good thing they hadn't arrived any later. He'd arranged their registration and they'd be officially there in a consultative capacity for his benefit. Mel nodded as if this was no surprise to her.

Koyane then launched into a brief resume of every member of the Korean, Japanese and other delegations who'd be present. By the third name, Luce had tuned out. He bit into a pastry filled with a red paste that tasted a little like the cakes from the night before. Not bad, he thought, as he finished his breakfast and prepared for a day of watching Mel at work. This would be an eye-opener for sure.

Forty-four

It was three days of the most boring negotiations ever. Even Mel had showed irritation for a few moments. Luce couldn't help but notice that she grew more tired as the hours passed, slumping in her seat as her eyelids dropped lower and lower. This was worse than when he'd been here on business — there weren't any gifts, drinks or interpreters, and his Japanese and Korean vocabulary combined would fit on the back of his hand.

Every time they broke for coffee, tea or

meals, Mel mingled among the diplomats, her sweet smile belying her exhaustion as she spoke. More than that, she listened. Luce didn't know what to do. He was useless in negotiations he didn't understand and Mel seemed to have everything under control, but he wanted to be near her. And the more he watched, the more he saw.

The businessmen, diplomats and government officials, who had nothing but cold politeness for him, actually listened to Mel. Her smile was genuine when she left one conversation for another, but the deference they treated her with was like nothing he'd ever experienced. Mel belonged in this world – how had he not noticed before? How could he have ever thought she was nothing but a lowly angel, fit only to be an office temp?

If he'd first met her in this sort of environment, where she strode among humans like their beloved queen, would he have even noticed her like he had in the office? Or would he have dismissed her as not worth the trouble? Would he have even been able to see that she was an angel? The terrifying thought froze his breath in his throat: to have seen her in action, doing what she was so eminently qualified to do, and to have missed out on the sheer joy that was Melody? Had he seen her in the past and ignored his salvation as she sailed by?

Patrick was right. He was watching the Domination of Earth, demonstrating to even the stupidest devil that she'd more than earned that title. And it looked so effortless, too — though he saw that the constant networking took its toll. These negotiations were wearing her down until he found himself suggesting she rest, return home, have some tea, sit down a moment, grab something to eat...oh, the list went on.

The exception was Han Dong-Suk. He actively avoided Mel, Luce noticed. The moment Mel entered a room, he left it. On the few occasions that they had spoken, the exchange was always curt and the man's expression seemed more stubborn than ever. Mel, on the other hand, lost her smile for the duration of the conversation and a few minutes afterwards. He didn't need to understand Korean to know that things were going badly for Mel with this man. How could an international agreement be derailed by just one, difficult person?

That evening, after much bowing and some Western hand-shaking, the delegations from Japan and Korea parted ways. From their stony faces, Luce assumed negotiations hadn't ended well. The moment the door of Koyane's car slammed shut behind her, Mel confirmed it by bursting into tears. Luce pulled her into his arms, but she was inconsolable and her tears flowed without cease until they reached Koyane's house. Holding her so close, Luce shared her pain, too. He felt her heart ripping asunder, witnessing her remembered pain as she burned alive in an inferno that could have passed for Hell…if he hadn't known it was a Japanese city.

"Mel, it's not going to be the same as it was during the Second World War. There aren't many people living on these islands – they're just uninhabitable rocks in the ocean. Just like the nuclear testing other countries have done on uninhabited islands in the past. Sure, they'll damage the islands and ecosystems and stuff, but it's not the same as a nuclear strike on a city." He felt Mel's pain twist as if someone had slid a knife into her heart. "What?"

"Mere-san walks the paths of the future. She knows better than any what the consequences of this decision will be," Koyane called from the driver's seat before he climbed out of the car.

Could the man be more cryptic? "Talk to me, Mel," Luce coaxed.

Mel sniffed and wiped her tears away. "Luce, what do you think will happen if North Korea detonates a nuclear weapon – or more than one – in Japanese territory?"

He felt himself grinning. This was a joke, surely. "But it's not Japanese territory. The Koreans say it's theirs and it has been for centuries."

Mel slowly shook her head. "No, Luce. The Koreans believe it's theirs and so do the Japanese. So imagine if a hydrogen bomb blew up contested Japanese territory. China, Russia, the United States and all their allies would sit up and take notice. And someone would retaliate against North Korea, who have more nuclear weapons."

Keiko laughed. "You're wasting your time explaining it to him, Murielle-sama. If he didn't understand immediately, he never will. This one's more brawn than brain. A true muscle man – pretty to look at, but no substance."

"Oh, I understand it," Luce snapped. "I just don't understand why you think any other country would send a nuke against a city, even if North Korea does detonate one of theirs on those rocks. I mean, humans aren't that stupid. Not even their governments are. They know what would happen."

"The man in charge of North Korea's arsenal doesn't," Mel said softly, the flood of tears starting again. "Han Dong-Suk knows nothing of Hiroshima or Nagasaki. And if foreign powers attacked his businesses, as his company builds and runs nuclear power plants throughout Korea, he wouldn't hesitate to retaliate. He's a man who doesn't care about public opinion – he makes his money in an industry that the world demonises. Sorry, Luce. He doesn't care if people hate him, as long as his businesses make money." She wrenched off her seatbelt.

Luce followed Mel into the house, still sharing her pain through her death grip on his hand. He wanted to wrap himself around her and heal all her hurt, but he had no idea where to start. Heartbreak wasn't like physical pain, with a physical cause that could be healed, even by an angel as clumsy as he was.

"You help just by being with me," Mel murmured, resting her head against his chest as she stepped out of her shoes.

"If your way doesn't work, my people have other means that are not as honourable by human terms." Keiko flashed a feral grin that made Luce think of sharks. No, definitely not human. He wondered if the girl ate humans or if she did something worse to them. His bet was on the nastier side that made cannibalism seem nice. "But humans are dishonourable by our people's standards, so I see no need to hold back on their account," she added.

Koyane held up his hand. "Murielle-sama has not admitted defeat yet, Keiko-san. We wait for her, as this would not be her first miracle."

Mel smiled through her tears. "Thank you for your confidence, Koyane, but any further action on my part will have to wait until morning. My heart is too heavy tonight to see through the darkness in this matter. Perhaps in the morning light my course will be clearer."

"Then let's go out for dinner and karaoke!" Keiko cried, clapping her hands as a wicked grin lit up her face. "Singing solves most problems, I find. I wish to hear Murielle-sama's voice and demonstrate mine."

Luce snorted. "You won't. Mel doesn't sing."

"Yes, I do in Japan, my love," Mel interjected. "Karaoke here in Tokyo is a much more private affair than in London. I think Keiko is in for an unpleasant surprise – I'm a terrible singer. But I wouldn't miss it for the world, if only for another amazing performance from Luce here." She lifted her teary eyes to meet his and he felt her yearning lace through the undercurrent of pain.

"Anything for you, Melody," he said.

Koyane jingled his keys. "I'll lock up the

garage, then."

Luce stared. "Aren't we going out?"

"Sure, Muscle Man, but we're walking," Keiko returned. "I would like to hear Murielle-sama's opinion on the lovely new tempura shop around the corner and the karaoke bar is only one street further. Driving home after karaoke is illegal in Japan!" She laughed as she led the way out to the street.

Humans had some crazy laws, then, Luce decided, following Mel.

Forty-five

The two women ordered drinks while Koyane and Luce picked up the song menus, then all four of them squeezed into a booth with worn vinyl sofas and a table scarred from what looked like decades of drinks.

"What did you order?" Luce asked. He'd tried a few Japanese beers and he didn't mind them, but this didn't look like the sort of place to have the top-shelf whisky he preferred.

"Ooh, a bit of everything," Keiko said airily. "Mere-san said this is your first proper karaoke, so no half-measures."

Mere-san? What was with the strange nicknames?

Mel kissed his cheek. "I promise you'll enjoy it, my love. And the drinks menu's on the wall by the intercom, so you can always order something else if you want." She waved at a poster that was covered in Japanese characters.

"Mel, I don't speak or read Japanese," he objected.

"Then trust me. Even if I can't persuade stubborn diplomats, I can read a drinks menu. And karaoke calls for cocktails." Her smile had returned, even if her pain lurked underneath. Could none of the others sense it – just him? A glance at Keiko's and Koyane's smiling faces gave him his answer.

"Mel," he began, then changed his mind and said, "Are you sure this is what you want?"

She slid along the blue vinyl until her leg pressed against his. "Yes. Just because the negotiations didn't go well, doesn't mean I must be miserable. There is still hope – there always is."

Her heavy heart made the words sound like

a lie. But Mel couldn't lie, which meant she believed it. She could be wrong, though…

Luce nodded, opening one of the music menus. Nothing but Japanese writing. He sighed and closed it again.

"Here's the English one, my love," Mel said, handing him a folder that looked exactly the same as the others. A quick glance at the first page told him she was right about this, at least. Well, mostly. He wondered if The Rowing Stones were a cover band, an unfortunate typo, or a comment on Mick Jagger's music. Maybe all three, he decided, using the remote to pick a few of their songs.

Keiko and Koyane had already keyed in their selections, so he wasn't surprised to see Keiko pick up a microphone and start singing something that he didn't understand a word of. She had such a lovely voice, though…far too lovely for a woman who said such unpleasant things the rest of the time. In fact…

Luce blinked as the microphone landed in his lap. He looked up. Where in Hell had all the drinks come from? The table was full of half-drunk cocktails and, as his gaze landed on each of them, his brain reminded him what they tasted like, as if he'd sampled them all.

Keiko cleared her throat. "I said your song, Muscle Man."

Luce stared at the screen. Britney Spears? No, he wouldn't have picked this. And he sure didn't remember picking anything after the first couple of Stones songs. "Sing it yourself or skip it," he snapped, throwing the microphone back. He glanced around for Mel, then realised that she was the warm weight sleeping against his side. How long had they been there? No longer than ten minutes, surely. Not enough for Mel to fall asleep! His watch told him he'd lost three hours. What the Hell?

Keiko's knowing look suggested she was responsible for his lapse in concentration, but Luce didn't know how. "Did you drug my drink?" he asked.

She laughed. "Stupid Muscle Man. I don't need to resort to poisons to control your mind. Though I did enjoy your little striptease as you revealed all the muscles. So did Mere-san."

Striptease? Not that he minded getting his

gear off, but missing Mel's reaction hit Luce hard. "Mel?" He patted her shoulder, trying to wake her.

"She won't wake until she chooses," Koyane said quietly. "Let her sleep. She is trying to find a way to a clear future that doesn't end in war. She said the future was too clouded for her to see."

War was inevitable? No wonder Mel was so heartbroken. Too many would die if war erupted here. Someone needed to tell that stupid human to stop what he intended to do. Divorce his weird wife and take up a hobby. Or find a sane girl. Well, he could help in the divorce department.

Luce rose, lifting Mel in his arms. "I'll take her home, then. I'm not letting Mel sleep on some sofa in a bar when she could be comfortable in bed."

Keiko looked put out, but Koyane simply nodded and held the door open for them.

A barrage of truly terrible singing assaulted him as soon as he entered the passage, but Luce used the cacophony as cover to whisper to Koyane, "What did she do?" He jerked his head at Keiko, who'd picked up the microphone again. "I only remember her starting to sing, then nothing."

Koyane's smile was bland. "Keiko is a siren, Lucifer-san, and a song is all she needs to ensnare a man's mind. Our kind are not normally susceptible, but you seem to be an exception. Ask Mere-san, for she will have more answers than I do." He stared at Mel, the same way Patrick had when he'd thought Luce wasn't looking. "Please take good care of her."

Luce gritted his teeth. "I always do."

He carried her back to Koyane's house, but he wasn't sure how to get his key into the lock without putting her down. And the dark, deserted street wasn't the best place for that.

"Mel," he began tentatively. "We're home. You fell asleep again, this time at the karaoke place. Any chance you can wake up and help me unlock the door?"

He waited, then leaned in and whispered her name again before he kissed her. He felt her smile before her eyes opened.

"What is it, Luce?"

"I need you to stand up or help me open the

door."

"Where are the keys?"

Luce jerked his head to the right. "My pocket."

Blood rushed to all the right places as Mel's fingers slipped into the depths of his hip pocket. She unlocked the door and together they opened it. He shuffled in sideways with her before setting her on the step. A few seconds of clumsy moonwalking and he'd managed to take his shoes off. Mel had slumped against the wall after removing one of her shoes, so Luce finished the job and lifted her again.

Elbowing aside the screens that barred his way, he laid her carefully on her futon and stretched out beside her. "Do you want me to help you change out of your clothes?"

"Mmm," she said, turning onto her side.

Luce laughed, then set to work on her blouse buttons. "Mel, can I ask you something?"

She sounded slightly more alert. "Of course, my love."

"What happened in the karaoke bar? Keiko

started singing and I woke up three hours later."

"Keiko is a siren. Her song controls men's minds. Women's, too, possibly. I'm not sure. I'd never seen her do it before. I had no idea it would affect you so strongly – neither Koyane nor I experienced such a response. She didn't force you to do anything except forget the time she had you under control, but I noticed that your responses were slower. She's angry because we wouldn't let her use her mind control at the meetings. She said she could have changed the outcome, but Koyane preferred to find a more lasting solution, and I agreed. Now…once I leave, Keiko has sworn she will act as she sees fit to protect the islands." Mel sighed. "I can't take away a human's free will, or Keiko's, if it comes down to it. So I'm trying to find another way, but I can't. I just can't, Luce."

Her smile had slipped away as tears surfaced again.

"If anyone can find a way to stop a nuclear war, it's you, Melody," he said. "I love you. No one else could save me but you, so I have every faith in you."

Her heart twinged again and Luce's did the same as he shared her pain. "Love can't fix everything, Luce. When a man like Mr Han's heart is broken because his wife refuses his affections, nothing will stop him until he manages to win her back. Mr Han's obsessive love for his wife is the reason we're here and the reason we failed. It can harm as much as it can heal – maybe more in this case."

"She told me he didn't want her. I guess she lies about a lot of things." Lying, manipulative bitch, Luce added in his head.

"No, Mr Han said she didn't want to sleep with him and he wasn't lying. He's doing this for her – for love, if you can believe it."

Someone needed to tell Han Dong-Suk that his wife wasn't worthy of his love – she was a kinky, cheating bitch who manipulated other men into having sex with her.

Luce tucked the quilt over Mel's naked body, wishing he could join her. "You just concentrate on getting some sleep. I've seen how exhausted you've been this week – you need rest."

Mel covered a yawn. "I know…but more important is finding a path through this mess. Such a clouded future…it's as if my being here is making the future impossible to see. Yet I've done nothing that could have far-reaching effects on the future of these two countries this trip. I've been worse than useless."

It wasn't her presence causing the clouded future, but his own, Luce was certain. He could fix this mess. He didn't need to see the future like Mel did to know that a messy divorce would keep a man occupied for a long time. That's why she'd brought him, right? To help? Then he would – the way he knew best.

"You're never useless. Just tired. Everything will look better in the morning," Luce promised.

He watched and waited while Mel's eyes slid shut and her breathing evened. When he was certain she was fast asleep, he rose and crept back to the entry for his shoes. If Mel didn't get to rest, no one else would, either. No one made Mel's life difficult with him around. Time to raise Hell in the Han household.

Forty-Six

Luce hammered on the door a third time. He didn't want to kick it in, but if he had to, he would.

He'd just raised his fist for a fourth try when the door flew open, framing Sunny in a kimono that gaped open at the front, revealing…perhaps one of the last sights he wanted to see.

"I saw you on the video monitor and I rushed down as fast as I could. You came to see me again! Come in, come in!" she gushed, grabbing his arm and trying to pull him inside.

He shook her off and strode past her into the darkened house. He almost tripped over the collection of shoes at the bottom of the steps. Shit, what was with the shoe-removing ritual here? Grumpily, Luce bared his socks and stomped up the steps into the house proper.

"Shh, come to my library," Sunny whispered. "I knew you'd come again. And I've been such a bad girl — I bought a new flogger. This one has little beads on it and I heard it's much better than my last one." She tugged on his arm again.

"Don't touch me, woman," he growled. "I'm here to speak to your husband. Wake him up. Now!"

"But we can't. If he finds out about us, he'll divorce me and I'll be a laughing stock. A marriage that only lasted a few months! I'll never be on reality TV again if that happens!" she wailed, falling to her knees. "Fuck me first. Then wake my husband up."

Luce stared down in disgust. "No. I'm here for business, not...that."

Footsteps approached and a switch clicked, flooding the reception room with light. A loud male voice barked something that Luce didn't understand.

Sunny stammered a reply in her irritating little-girl voice.

"Who are you?" Mr Han boomed.

"Luce Iblis, CEO of the HELL Corporation," he said smoothly, extending a hand as he approached the man. Mr Han ignored it. "We met at a reception here earlier in the week."

"What are you doing in my house after midnight?"

Luce looked him in the eye. "Why don't you ask your cheating wife that, Mr Han? She invited me in." He couldn't lie, but this at least was true. He hoped the man would take the hint.

"He said he was here on important business!" Sunny insisted.

Both men stared at the skinny, scantily-clad girl lying on the floor. "So why are you nearly naked, then?" Mr Han asked. Luce knew the look of a man trying to hide his lust — he'd done it himself often enough. Now, all he was trying to hide was nausea.

"Show him the video," Luce ordered, leading the way to the woman's licentious library. "I know you took one. Show him that the reason you're not sleeping with him is because you prefer to fuck other men on your desk." Sunny's face clouded with anger. "I said show him!" Luce roared.

She skittered around to her tablet and flicked it on, chewing on an intricately painted fingernail as she waited for it to boot. A few swipes of her finger and she thrust the device at Mr Han. "There! See what a truly powerful man can do!" she screeched at her husband.

As her recorded voice started yelping, Luce felt bile rising in his throat. He didn't want to hear it again – once was enough. And the memory was nicely faded – had Keiko's mind tricks helped with that, too? Maybe he'd thank her for it when he got back. He pulled a business card out of his pocket. "You're causing a political incident for a woman who doesn't love you and openly mocks you in your own house. I don't think she's worth lighting a cheap birthday candle for, let alone a nuclear pyre to consume an entire island. If you want to speak to me again, here's my card. I don't need to see this. This is a private matter between you and your cheap whore of a wife." He turned on his heel and headed for the front door.

"How dare you!" Sunny shrieked, tackling from behind. But even throwing her entire weight at him didn't do much, so she tried again.

Luce kept going until he reached the steps and his shoes. He didn't want to stay long enough to put them on – he'd rather walk barefoot. Sighing, he reached down to yank off one sock, then the other.

"I'll never let you fuck me again!" she screeched.

Luce turned his head so she could see his indifference. "Good."

"Good? Good? HA! You'll never have a better woman than me!"

"I have a better woman than you. A thousand…no, a million times better than you. The only reason I paid you any attention at all is because she wanted me to make sure you enjoyed your evening while she talked business with your husband."

Shock turned Sunny's face white. She gaped like a goldfish for a few seconds before she snapped her mouth shut. "It's that blonde bitch, isn't it? Keiko's consultant. Well, if you're going to spoil my marriage, then I'll spoil any chance you ever had with her. I'll send her the video my husband's watching and we'll see how much she wants you when she knows you flogged another woman into submission and then forced her to have sex with you." She whipped her phone out of her pocket and started punching numbers.

It was Luce's turn to stare in shock. If Mel saw the video, she'd leave him for sure. She wouldn't believe it was just an act, him doing what he'd done a hundred thousand times before, even if this last time had been for her. He'd made it look and sound real to get on Sunny's good side. He shouldn't have wasted his time. Mel would believe he'd returned to his demonic ways and she'd leave him, because she didn't do demons. Then he realised, "You don't have her number and she wouldn't give it to you, anyway. Not even your husband has it, because Mel wouldn't take him for a client." He grinned reflexively in relief.

"Maybe not, but I have Keiko's number and she'll show her for me. Keiko is my friend."

Luce's heart sank. If anyone hated him more than this bitch, it was mind-controlling Keiko. She'd show Mel for sure and laugh the whole time, too.

"Do whatever you like." He walked out, hearing the door click closed behind him. Once the house was out of sight, he picked up the pace. He had to get back before Mel woke up and saw the video or…oh God. He'd lose her forever.

Forty-Seven

As Mel watched Luce leave the Hans' house, she breathed a spiritual sigh of relief. For a moment, the streetlight outside brightened, then dimmed again: the only sign of her presence in her spirit form. At her full power, she could make a nuclear blast look like nothing, but Mel was tired and it showed. She hoped this would be the last night she'd need to walk the paths of the future for a while. This crisis hadn't come at a good time. She knew she was fading and if she didn't rest soon

– either here or in Heaven – her soul would drop below the energy level she needed to maintain this body, and Heaven would be her only option. Her weakened soul would be powerless to resist Heaven's siren call – far stronger than anything Keiko could do – and that was as it should be. Better that Heaven drew souls home before they faded entirely.

She felt another pull now, too: that of her soul's bond with Luce. Mel yearned to follow him home so she could embrace and congratulate him on his choice of actions tonight. She should have spotted that Sun-Hee's liking for Luce ran far deeper than a simple preference. Luce was recovering from Sun-Hee's onslaught, though – Mel had taken time and care to ensure that he did. Energy that perhaps some would say Mel should have saved for herself, in her depleted state, but Luce was too important to neglect. She loved him and he deserved all the help she could give him.

Just a few minutes…and she could feel his arms around her body as he held her. Oh, so tempting…but no. Mel knew she had work to do. Once her task was complete, then she could enjoy an idyll with Luce in Koyane's house outside Kyoto. She just needed to know for sure that the future was clear and not the war she feared.

Concentrating hard, Mel reached for the time strands of the present, tracing them into the infinite futures that could eventuate from this moment. What had appeared to be a spiderweb in a fog was now haloed in water droplets that glistened in the clear morning light. Ah, that one – the strand broader and brighter than the others. She hummed with laughter at her use of human words for a concept no human could understand. Now, all she had to do was follow it and investigate all of its branches to ensure that this path to war had been blocked, or at least rendered highly improbable.

She felt the charged energy of dawn touch her body and knew her time was up. She'd checked most of the threads and she was almost certain everything was woven together in a more harmonious pattern now. Well, except in the Han household. That…was a sad case, but humans could make bad choices in anything, including love.

She slid her way back into her body, sensing the sluggishness of her overworked soul. This time, she swore she'd rest. She'd enlist Luce's help and together they'd recover in Kyoto. She couldn't wait to show him the ancient hot spring she and Koyane had first discovered there. She suspected Koyane had spoken privately to the local Dynameis to ensure that earthquakes and volcanic activity wouldn't adversely affect the flow of the spring, but she'd never called him out about it. As far as guilty pleasures went, this was about as benign as her penchant for tea.

Although she was usually such a morning person, today, she was anything but. Her body didn't seem to want to respond and it was such an effort just to force her eyelids apart. Too much fussing, she chided herself. She should have only looked at the most likely futures and left it there, instead of traipsing through every tiny path of each infinitesimally small possibility to its eventual end. When she woke, she'd tell Luce and he'd laugh at her. But he'd help her recover, too, better than anyone else could. That's why she'd expended so much energy and let her soul become as drained as it had: she knew he'd be there to care for her. All she had to do was return to him and everything would be all right.

Mel focussed on her body's breathing — usually the easiest way to assume control of it again. No more travelling far from her body until she'd recovered, she scolded herself, or she'd end up in Heaven and have to rebuild her body when she came home. She'd better warn Luce just in case, though. He hadn't taken it well the last time her body disintegrated outside Heaven's gates.

Right. Time to wake and pack her things so they could leave for Kyoto. Maybe she'd even see Fujiyama on her train trip south. If the clouds and haze weren't hiding the summit, of course, which happened far too often in this highly industrialised country.

Mel blinked, stretching slowly to stave off the stiffness of having slept so long. She became aware of the absence of Luce's arms and it was such a lonely feeling. She'd grown so used to sleeping in his embrace that the morning seemed cold without him. Ah, after such a worrying night, he was probably nursing a coffee in the kitchen, dreading the discussion that would follow Keiko's discovery of a video Mel never intended to watch. She knew more than enough about what Luce had done, for she'd seen his memories through the lens of his own disgust and self-loathing. He'd come so far from the demon he once was. If it wasn't such a condescending concept, she'd be proud of him for conquering the demon of his past.

As for Mrs Han…Mel sighed as she rose and slipped on a robe. The woman would have slept with someone soon enough, she was that dissatisfied. Perhaps Luce had saved some poor human's soul from damnation by his sacrifice. Though given his experience, he'd probably spoiled the woman for anyone else.

The kitchen was empty, so she busied herself making tea and toast. She hadn't had a coffee since leaving London and she was profoundly glad that she'd managed to avoid a caffeine addiction for so long, what with

Luce's kindness in making a cup for her whenever he made one for himself. She never had the heart to refuse his offerings. She knew he was trying to be good, but sometimes the poor devil had no idea how to behave well in human or angelic society. It was a tribute to his heart, soul and fierce stubbornness that he persevered, though.

Her sigh rippled the surface of her cup of tea, diffusing the steam until it vanished into the air. Mel had just taken her first mouthful of toast when Keiko breezed in, radiating contentment as she wished Mel good morning. The siren stopped to stare at Mel. "Mere-san, is that a bruise or is it just jam on your cheek?"

Mel brushed at her cheek and her fingers came away sticky. "Plum jam, I think. Oops, I should be more careful." She headed for the sink to clean the stuff from her face, then returned to the table. "How are you feeling after last night, Keiko?"

Keiko grinned. "Much better this morning, Mere-san. Koyane was right. You do work miracles." She laid the newspaper on the table. The picture on the front depicted two businessmen shaking hands, with a tired but smiling Koyane in the background.

Mel lifted the paper so she could read it better. "Last night? Only a few hours ago! They sure moved fast. It's a wonder they didn't wait until morning. I bet rousing all those delegates from bed took some doing."

Keiko shrugged. "I wouldn't know. Apparently, Mr Han insisted he'd had a change of heart. Koyane got the call while we were still at the karaoke bar that he was needed to witness the signing. It seems they'd already written several versions, in anticipation that some agreement would be formulated, so it was an easy matter of obtaining the relevant signatures and the islands are my people's again. I wonder what changed his mind."

Mel raised her eyebrows as she dropped the newspaper. "I believe Mr Han had a falling out with his wife. Relinquishing the islands is his idea of revenge. So what are they called now? And which country owns them?"

"Neither and both, same as before. The only agreement they reached is on who will police and regulate fishing there, and my company's project just gained the exclusive licence for the place. They can argue over the rocks all they want, but as long as I control the ocean and all that is in it, the islands and their waters will be safe."

The oceans and all that was in it? Mel tried not to react to the girl's slip, but she suspected the siren wasn't a girl at all, not if she admitted to holding such power. The chance remark placed her as one of her people's elders.

"Where's Lucifer this morning?" Keiko asked, scanning the kitchen as if she expected him to be hiding in a corner.

It was Mel's turn to shrug. "I'm not sure. He was up earlier than me, so I haven't seen him yet today."

"Good," the siren said, pulling out her phone. "I think I know why we've had so much trouble this week. Instead of charming Han Dong-Suk and Sun-Hee, he's been turning them hostile." She held the phone out to Mel. "Sun-Hee sent me this video of him. You shouldn't trust him, Mere-san."

The sound of a small dog yelping, followed by Luce's emotionless voice delivering lines that he hated almost as much as he hated himself for saying them, broke her heart. She swiped the video message off and returned the phone to Keiko. "Thank you, but I don't need to see it. I know the gist of what Luce did and why. And I trust him just as much as he deserves." She rose and took her dishes to the sink to wash up.

"Murielle-sama, have I done something to offend you? If I have, then I am deeply sorry," Keiko said, her voice suddenly quiet.

Mel stacked her dishes neatly in the dryer. "No, I'm just worried about Luce." She reached for his soul and found nothing. She stretched further, but found her vision failing. Too weak. Mel grabbed the counter to stop herself from falling. She couldn't search for him like she normally would, so she decided to do things the human way. If he'd gone out, his shoes would be gone. A quick peep into the tiny entrance hall confirmed it. Luce's shoes weren't there. Well, it was daylight and he was hardly incapable of defending himself – he'd probably gone for a walk. Maybe to get more pastries before she woke up. Mel smiled. That would be so like Luce – sweetening her up before breaking his news about what he'd done last night.

She headed up the stairs to get dressed for the day.

It wasn't until she made the bed, rolling up the futons to keep them out of the way, that she found his note.

Mel read it twice, took a deep breath, and checked the cupboard. Empty. Luce's clothes were gone. His luggage, too.

Tears rolled down her cheeks.

She fingered the letters that only a man who'd learned to write by carving them into stone would produce:

I'M SORRY I DISAPPOINTED YOU.

I'VE GONE BACK TO HELL WHERE I BELONG.

A light tap on the door made her lift her head.

Koyane cleared his throat. "Mere-san, I wish to know whether you and Lucifer would prefer lunch bento from here, or from the shinkansen station. I'm sending Keiko to get some more manju, so I thought I'd ask her to…" He caught sight of her expression and his mouth hung open for a moment before he recollected himself. "What is wrong?"

Mel swallowed. "It's Luce. He's gone home."

Then she blacked out.

Forty-eight

It had taken both Keiko and Koyane to get Mel to the train station and settled in her first-class seat after Koyane had revived her. They seemed to hover beside her for the whole trip to Kyoto, and Mel was grateful for their care. She hadn't been this weak in a long time and she was afraid of exposing her true nature if she lost consciousness again.

A taxi transported them from the station to Koyane's house, where she immediately retired to her room. Keiko brought her dinner and informed her that Koyane had offered the use of the hot springs and the miraculous cure they provided. Mel happily accepted, for she knew better than anyone that the stories of miracles were true.

Mel closed her eyes as she lathered up the shower gel before smoothing it over her skin. Japanese communal bathing seemed the most natural thing in the world when she was here, though it was hardly communal when she had the empty bathhouse all to herself.

"Mere-san, would you like me to wash your back?"

Ah, not quite empty.

Keiko's eager smile beamed at her beneath her cherry-coloured knot of hair. "It would be my pleasure, Mere-san."

Mel shook her head slowly as she dipped her bowl into the steaming onsen water. "Thank you, Keiko, but I'm almost finished." She tipped the bowl and poured hot water down her back. Several cascades later, Mel rose from her crouch and stepped toward the murky pool.

"If it is too hot for you, Mere-san, there is a

cold tap over there." Keiko pointed with a long, scarlet fingernail.

Mel laughed gently and submerged in the ancient, spring-fed pool. The heat permeated her very bones, releasing her tension and a blissful sigh.

"If there is anything you wish for, you have only to name it and I will give it to you. Koyane, too." Keiko slid gracefully into the pool beside Mel. "You have the most exquisite breasts. I'm not surprised your muscle man stared at them so much."

"My muscle man? Do you mean Luce?"

Keiko nodded.

"Why do you call him that?"

The girl shrugged. "The muscles are his most prominent feature. He evidently thinks with one of them, for his mind is nothing to admire. His actions in Tokyo confirmed it." Keiko's eyes tightened with hurt, as if she'd known the betrayal of many men. Mel wondered how old the youthful-looking siren really was. She'd heard stories of sirens living for centuries. "You have enslaved him without needing the songs of my people. That implies a feeble mind. What use is such a one to you?"

Mel's heart sank. Luce wasn't easy to explain to another angel, let alone this strange siren. "Luce and I share more than may be evident on the surface. Beneath the muscles are hidden depths I doubt even he is aware of. As for his body…" Mel licked her lips, hoping she could find the right words. "Luce knows my desires and he sculpts his body accordingly."

Keiko's giggles made her sound much younger than she looked. "You brought Muscle Man as your bed toy? Oh, so that's why you sent him away – for seducing that hag at the banquet! Now it makes sense. I would be honoured to take his place for as long as you need me, Mere-san." Her eyes shone in anticipation.

"Luce left of his own accord and I will follow him as soon as I'm strong enough," Mel said gently. "As Koyane will tell you, I rest alone, though I thank you for your very kind offer." The girl's face crumpled and Mel quickly added, "Surely you don't find me that irresistible. If you could choose your perfect partner, what would she be like?"

Keiko closed her eyes and breathed deeply. "She would have power, greater than or equal to what I possess. A body with rounder curves than mine. My favourite colours are those of fire, so her hair and her fins would be shades of flame. And she would be both kind and brave enough to risk her life and her people for me, if I were placed in danger." Keiko sighed deeply.

Mel grasped the girl's hand, slipping into the surface layers of her soul. The watery image of a fiery redhead against…ice?…with eyes as blue as the ocean's depths appeared and faded. The girl Keiko spoke of was no fantasy – she was real. "You speak as if you have already met her. What's her name?"

Keiko laughed shakily. "I do not know. She saved my life and swam away without a word. My brother says it's silly to dwell on such a fleeting contact – I must have imagined the girl, not to mention any feelings I might have for her. Red is the rarest colour among my kind. I've heard it was something only those of the Black line possess, and then only if there is Black ancestry on both sides. That line is all but extinct in our ocean and it is the same in the Atlantic. I can dye my hair, my lips and my nails, but my fins tell the truth." Keiko's feet broke the surface of the water, but they were no longer recognisable as human appendages. Her tail flukes extended well past the bones of her toes, a delicate fan of emerald green. "She can only belong to the people of the Indian Ocean, a people so distant I hear stories of a lost Black dragon found there. Have you heard rumours of a fire-coloured mermaid in the Indian Ocean during your time there?"

Mel shook her head. "There are few rumours about your kind there at all. They are as adept at hiding as the people of your ocean. I've only met one of them, but that was such a long time ago…yet I do remember she left to follow a red-haired man. Coincidence, perhaps, but who can say?" She hoisted herself out of the steaming pool and left wet footprints on the wooden slats to her clothes. "Thank you for your kindness and your confidence. I need rest, so I bid you good night, Keiko-san." Mel dressed and headed out of the bathhouse into the cool night air.

She paused to change from bath slippers to outdoor shoes for the short walk through the moonlit formal garden. Her house slippers waited inside, lined with something soft and fluffy. She was Koyane's honoured guest, but she didn't use guest slippers – he kept this special pair for her. She padded quietly to the kitchen, shivering a little as the rice paper screens did little to protect her from the falling temperature outside.

Koyane was waiting, as she knew he would be. He poured two cups of tea and pushed one across the table toward the empty place across from him. "Do you feel better now?"

Mel smiled and sat, inhaling the steam from her handleless cup. "I do, thank you. The waters from your hot spring work miracles."

"Not as brilliantly as you do. I still can't believe you managed to get Han to make the right decision, though for the wrong reasons. There are a lot of people in Korea and Japan who will breathe easier for a time because of you. Thank you."

Mel's gaze dropped to her cup. Luce had made it happen, not her, yet he wasn't here to celebrate his victory. She said nothing for a few seconds as she sipped her tea and wished the miracle spring could have washed away her exhaustion, too. Her body badly needed sleep.

"Did Keiko join you? I told her you wished to be alone, but I believe her excitement at your presence has overwhelmed her sense of courtesy. You'd think she was still a child, she's so thrilled to be around you."

Mel swallowed. "How old is Keiko?"

Koyane smiled broadly. "Would you believe me if I told you she is close to a century?"

Recalling the knowledge in the girl's shining eyes as she voiced her strongly held views on men, Mel nodded. "Is she one of the elders in her ocean?"

"Yes. One of the most influential, too, so it's amusing to see her fawning over you. A woman who holds more power than she does – I'm surprised she didn't beg to share your mat tonight."

"She offered," Mel admitted, "but while I'm close to her ideal, she's met someone who is closer to it than I will ever be. A red-haired girl, one of her kind, she said. I guess I'm lucky

I don't have red hair, or she wouldn't be able to resist me at all." She dropped her gaze. "Besides, what I need is rest and not companionship tonight."

Koyane's eyes darkened with concern. "So Patrick said. He asked me to watch you carefully for signs that you have done too much. He wanted me to remind your companion, too, to take care of you every moment, but I didn't manage to catch him before he left. I admit, I found what Patrick said very difficult to believe. You have spent time in Heaven and an extended stay in Western Australia, where I know you keep a retreat. What has worn you out so much?"

"Work. Raphael had a demon problem in Western Australia. I helped him take care of it, but at great personal cost."

"And…the fallen angel who travelled with you? Was he part of the problem? Is he still?"

Mel shook her head slowly. "Raphael thought he was, but the politics of Hell turned out to be more complex than I'd realised. It also seems that a fallen angel might not have fallen, had he not been pushed at the point of a flaming sword." She closed her eyes. "Luce…is a complete contradiction. A risen angel and a redeemed demon, yet still the Lord of Hell. And a surprisingly caring man whose soul speaks eloquently to mine. It's been centuries since I've mentored anyone, yet who else understands him well enough to provide the support he needs to find his place among us again? He has been betrayed by too many angels in the past to trust easily." She finished her tea and allowed Koyane to pour her another cup.

"If what Patrick says is true, and I have seen the evidence with my own eyes this morning, the only thing you should be doing now is resting. If you are the only one he trusts, I'm sure he can wait until you have recovered before resuming his training with you." Koyane's worried eyes never left hers as he took a deep draught of tea. He set his cup down and extended his hand. "Please, will you permit me to see?"

Mel nodded and pressed her palm against his. She felt the gentle touch of Koyane's soul brushing the edges of hers, but she relaxed and concentrated on enjoying her tea. She had no secrets to hide.

After several minutes, Koyane released her hand and held her gaze instead. "You must already know that you are even more drained than you were in London. Barely a shimmer is left of the blinding light I have seen whenever you have allowed my touch in the past. Please permit me the honour of restoring you, as you did after the Second World War. My home, my bathhouse, everything I own is yours to aid your recovery. Tell me what you need and it is yours."

Mel summoned a smile. "Right now, all I'd like is a cup of milk and some sleep. In the morning, over breakfast, we can discuss a future past tonight."

Koyane bowed. "As you wish." He rose and headed for the fridge. Time ticked as he stared at the contents before he turned to Mel. "We only have soy milk — no cow's milk. I completely forgot to buy any. I can send Keiko out first thing tomorrow for some. Will you have the soy now, or would you prefer something different?"

"Soy is fine." Mel yawned, barely tasting the cold liquid as she gulped it down. With Koyane's assistance, she stumbled to her room. Barely a minute after her body had stretched out on the futon, the angel was asleep.

Forty-nine

"Oh God, Melody, I'm so sorry. So sorry." Luce's agonised voice cut through Mel's consciousness and cleaved her heart. "Melody…"

Her soul reached for him, hoping to soothe some of the pain. Somehow, their bond bridged the distance so that she could sense him as if he were in the next room and not on the far side of a different continent.

Darkness and despair. Mel tried to surface from the depths of his soul to his thoughts.

Faintly, she smelled her own perfume and followed the scent. It was under Luce's nose, though mixed with cotton and laundry detergent. His arms crushed something soft to his chest and the fragrance intensified.

"God, what I'd give for it to be you in my arms again. I'm sorry, Melody. I'll do anything to make it up to you."

Pillow. He was holding her pillow and he'd sprayed her perfume on it before burying his face in the cotton cover.

"I love you, Luce," Mel heard her own laughing voice say. Luce's soul swelled with a cocktail of love and despair, allowing Mel to see the blurry video on his big-screen TV through his eyes. He hadn't been taking pictures at the Hans' party – he'd recorded a video on his phone.

The short video replayed from the beginning. She heard Luce complimenting her appearance and begging to be allowed to take photos so he could remember her when they were apart. His emotional state rollercoastered from joy to piercing despair.

"And I love you, Luce," her recorded self

repeated.

Mel would have gasped at the sharp pain penetrating his soul so deeply that it pierced hers, but she couldn't make a sound. She wanted to reassure him and tried projecting the soothing love within her own soul, but he didn't seem to sense her at all.

His arms tightened around the pillow and she felt her own despair when he dragged up the memory of losing her at Heaven's gates. Her body fading in his arms as it lost substance when her soul deserted the damaged shell. Luce was linking the past to his belief that he'd lost her again through his own misguided actions. "Melody..."

Mel jerked awake, unable to stand Luce's pain. She needed to be home with him. Hot springs be damned. He needed her. And, though it surprised her to admit it, she needed him. Not Koyane, not Patrick, not anyone else – only Luce.

The grey pre-dawn light filtered through the screens as Mel made her way to the kitchen. She set up her laptop and made tea while it powered up.

When she turned to check the laptop, her eyes met Koyane's grave gaze. "I need to go home, my friend."

"You need rest, Murielle-sama," he responded.

"I cannot rest here while Luce needs me elsewhere."

"Why can't your fallen angel wait for you to recover? What is so urgent? New angels can wait months before a proper mentor is assigned to them. Why is he so special?"

"Luce isn't a new angel. He's the redeemed Lord of Hell and a former demon. He's spent as many centuries corrupting souls as I have saving them and he believes he belongs with them. He's trying – you have no idea how hard he's trying – but it's miraculous that he can even break that many millennia of indoctrination to become what he is now. The longer I leave him without a mentor, the more likely it is that he'll retreat to Hell and revert to what he used to be. And I will have to go in after him, because no one else will. I won't lose his soul to the darkness, Koyane. He used to be one of the most powerful angels in Heaven and he's earned the right to stand among us once more, and the opportunity to rise again if that is his desire. I will not let my weakness lose that for him."

A solitary tear trickled down Koyane's nose as he bowed deeply. "Your love and sacrifice is an honour he does not deserve, Murielle-sama."

Mel swallowed with difficulty. "It is no sacrifice. Even if it were, it wouldn't be the first time." She wouldn't let Luce lose her again. She alone understood what it did to him. He didn't deserve the pain.

"Permit me to arrange your flights while you rest and pack your things." Mel nodded and he sat down at her laptop. His fingers ticked across the keys and a travel website appeared on the screen.

Mel set her empty cup on the table beside him and headed back to her room. She quickly packed her few belongings before stretching out on the futon for a moment's rest. When she landed, she intended to persuade the devil to take a holiday from Hell.

Heaven help her.

ABOUT THE AUTHOR

Demelza Carlton has always loved the ocean, but on her first snorkelling trip she found she was afraid of fish.

She has since swum with sea lions, sharks and sea cucumbers and stood on spray drenched cliffs over a seething sea as a seven-metre cyclonic swell surged in, shattering a shipwreck below.

Demelza now lives in Perth, Western Australia, the shark attack capital of the world.

The *Ocean's Gift* series was her first foray into fiction, followed by her suspense thriller *Nightmares* trilogy. She swears the *Mel Goes to Hell* series ambushed her on a crowded train and wouldn't leave her alone.

Want to know more? You can follow Demelza on Facebook, Twitter, YouTube or her website, Demelza Carlton's Place at:

www.demelzacarlton.com

Books by Demelza Carlton

Siren of Secrets series

Ocean's Secret (#1)
Ocean's Gift (#2)
Ocean's Infiltrator (#3)

Siren of War series

Ocean's Justice (#1)
Ocean's Widow (#2)
Ocean's Bride (#3)
Ocean's Rise (#4)
Ocean's War (#5)
How To Catch Crabs

Nightmares Trilogy

Nightmares of Caitlin Lockyer (#1)
Necessary Evil of Nathan Miller (#2)
Afterlife of Alana Miller (#3)

Mel Goes to Hell series

The Devil's Work (#1)
See You in Hell (#2)
Mel Goes to Hell (#3)
To Hell and Back (#4)
The Holiday From Hell (#5)
All Hell Breaks Loose (#6)
The Devil Goes to Heaven (#7)

Romance Island Resort series

Maid for the Rock Star (#1)
The Rock Star's Email Order Bride (#2)
The Rock Star's Virginity (#3)
The Rock Star and the Billionaire (#4)
The Rock Star Wants A Wife (#5)
The Rock Star's Wedding (#6)
Maid for the South Pole (#7)
Jailbird Bride (#8)

Romance a Medieval Fairytale series

Enchant: Beauty and the Beast Retold
Dance: Cinderella Retold
Fly: Goose Girl Retold
Revel: Twelve Dancing Princesses Retold
Silence: Little Mermaid Retold
Awaken: Sleeping Beauty Retold
Embellish: Brave Little Tailor Retold
Appease: Princess and the Pea Retold
Blow: Three Little Pigs Retold
Return: Hansel and Gretel Retold
Wish: Aladdin Retold
Melt: Snow Queen Retold
Spin: Rumpelstiltskin Retold
Kiss: Frog Prince Retold
Reflect: Snow White Retold
Roar: Goldilocks Retold
Cobble: Elves and the Shoemaker Retold